TRAILS' END

TRAILS' END

Paul Krebill
Enjoy!
2014

PAUL KREBILL

To order additional copies of this book, contact:
Xlibris LLC
1-888-795-4274
www.Xlibris.com
Orders@Xlibris.com
552069

PART I

Meeting

Ellis Island 1894

In 1894 a ship bound for Ellis Island carried, among its many immigrants, Gabriele Capone of Castellmmare di Stabia, Italy, and his wife,Teresina Raiola, a native of Angri, Italy, who would become the parents of Alphonse, born in New York City, the ninth of their children. In time, others from the southwest of Italy would join Al Capone in his nefarious activities in Chicago in the 1920s. Among these immigrants was Frank Nitto, who would succeed Big Al as leader of the Mob after Capone was sent away to prison. Nitti, as he was commonly called, had also come from Angri.

CHAPTER 1

Chicago 1927

A young woman dressed in a calf-length dress, rather plain, came out of the door of her apartment building on West Monroe Street and stepped out onto the sidewalk to begin her short walk north to Madison Street. She went to the end of the block and entered a neighborhood soda fountain and sandwich shop. Next to the shop entrance there was a doorway, presumably leading to the row of second floor apartment units above the shops along the street. She had been employed evenings at the counter a couple of months earlier. During this time, she had not really thought much about the apartments upstairs, having never had any reason—or permission-- to go up there. She had, however, noticed that on many evenings a rather steady stream of men had entered that door and she could hear them mounting the stairway. Her boss, Gert, lived in an apartment upstairs, but she used an inside stairway at the back of the shop. Gert was almost always upstairs after six o'clock or so, leaving Eleanor to handle the fountain. She served young people from the neighborhood during the afternoons, but during the evenings the customers were older folk apparently from the neighborhood..

One evening, an older man came in with his adult son. Apparently the younger man had just gotten back from Montana. He was excited about what he had found there. "There is a lot of work available in the western part of the state because there are still some productive gold mines in that area. So there are towns where you can get work. Jobs like store clerking, housekeeping and that sort of thing."

"Where in the state are these opportunities?" his father wondered.

"These days, out near Butte and on west to Missoula, little towns like Illinois City just east of Missoula. . . that was started by some folks from Illinois, I think."

Eleanor's imagination was stimulated by what she heard. She would remember another particular evening when three men dressed in black suits and overcoats wearing fedoras came into the shop. One of the men wore a white felt hat while smoking a cigar. He seemed to be the leader of the group as they walked past the counter and found their way to a table toward the back. As soon as they had entered the shop, Gert came down the stairs and went up to them and welcomed them. "What brings you boys to my establishment? I am honored!"

The main man took his cigar out of his mouth. "I've got some business to talk to these guys."

"Yes, sir"

When they sat down, Eleanor came to their table to take orders. "What can we get you?"

"Just coffee," the boss ordered. "And then we want to be alone and undisturbed. So just bring a coffee pot for any refills. We'll do the pouring."

Gert then turned to Eleanor. "And, Eleanor, this will be on the house. . . You can just stay up front."

Later, after they left the shop, Gert whispered to Eleanor. "Know who that was?"

"No. Looked important, though."

"That was Big Al and a couple of his underlings."

"Who?"

"The owner of this joint, and a lot of other stuff in Chicago. Al Capone."

This was only the beginning of what Eleanor would learn of Al Capone.

Eleanor was surprised one evening when Gert came downstairs around eight o'clock and took her seat on a stool at the counter. She summoned Eleanor to come and talk to her. "How would you like to make more money working for me?" she began.

"Yes, ma'am, I'd like to."

"Good, I've got Ginny coming in tomorrow to take the counter while I show you what I'd like for you to do. A job that will pay lots more."

"Well, I'm curious. Can you explain this new position?"

"No, I'd rather show you tomorrow night."

"Well, alright."

Eleanor had no idea what Gert had in mind and she was, of course, wondering. *I hope I can do it. I need more money.*

The next night Ginny showed up and took over, while Gert came down and led Eleanor up the back stairs. As the two walked down the second floor hallway they met a young man about Eleanor's age to whom Gert greeted him as he entered one of the doors along the hall. Gert's door was next to it. She ushered her young employee into her apartment and closed the door. Gert invited Eleanor to be seated in an easy chair, while Gert took the one across from it.

When she was seated, Eleanor asked, "Was that his apartment?"

"Well, no." Gert then explained to Eleanor about the apartment and about the second floor activities.

A cold shiver went down Eleanor's spine as she responded. "I see."

Gert then continued. "Now, that is what I wanted to talk to you about. I would like to invite you to take a position up here. I will pay you according to the number of people you see. She discussed the amount per client and then added. "And in addition, you can move from your present apartment and move into one of the rooms here, which will be yours rent free.

Eleanor was shocked, and it made her sick to her stomach. Gert asked her. "Do you have any questions?"

Eleanor could hardly speak but managed to say, "No."

"Think about it. You can let me know tomorrow morning if you want the job." With that, the two left the apartment and went downstairs to the soda fountain. "Ginny's here now, so you can go home for the night and let me know tomorrow."

That night in her own apartment, Eleanor felt sullied by what her boss had suggested. She could not get the whole idea out of her mind. She was bothered by what she had been told. She had never imagined anything as sordid. It made her feel ashamed even to work in the same building at the soda fountain.

She took a hot bath and went to bed, but did not sleep very well. Upon awakening, she knew her answer had to be an emphatic "NO."

When she approached the soda fountain, a police car was outside with its signal light on and its engine idling. A police officer was sitting in the driver's seat as a second policeman came out of the door from the upstairs and he shouted into the car "Call the ambulance. I think we have a homicide."

Eleanor entered the shop shaken and asked the custodian who was sweeping the floor. "What happened?"

"I dunno. Another shooting I guess. . . one of the girls."

With that, Eleanor felt faint, but had enough control to turn around, head out the door and ran home to her apartment. After collapsing for a few minutes in an overstuffed chair, she arose and began to pack her clothes in a small suitcase. Her money, which she had saved was hidden in a plain envelope at the bottom of her underwear drawer. Fortunately she was paid up on her rent. She left her door unlocked and put her house keys on the kitchen counter. She grabbed her suitcase and hurried over to Madison Street and boarded a street car which would take her downtown to Union Station. While riding, an idea began to take shape. She walked into the impressive depot and walked up to the information desk. After inquiring, she found her way to the Northern Pacific ticket counter.

She went to the window. "I'd like a ticket for Missoula, Montana."

When she got the ticket, she then found the gate number which had been given to her. Soon her train was announced and she joined the line of passengers walking out alongside the train which had just arrived under a semi-outdoor canopy. She showed her ticket to a conductor waiting outside one of the cars. "Second coach ahead, Ma'am."

Seated in a tall coach seat next to a window with her bag stowed in the overhead rack, she tried to relax and said a silent prayer. Soon the passenger train eased into motion and left the confines of Union Station heading west, leaving the outskirts of Chicago in its wake. The phrase which crowded every other thought from the young woman's mind was *good riddance.* But she would find to her dismay that the sordid situation would re-appear in her mind every so often, sometimes with the hideous sight of blood on the girl and her violated and murdered body covered with a dirty sheet.

As the North Coast Limited powerfully propelled its way west, Eleanor Helm began to feel the cleansing effect of the rural scenery as it passed by her window. The farms, surrounded by livestock had a calming influence upon Eleanor's mind and heart.

Meanwhile a black Cadillac sedan drove along Michigan Avenue and pulled up to the six storied Metropole Hotel on the corner of 23rd Street and Mchigan. Two men dressed in black suits got out and opened the rear door to usher out a third man with a cigar in his mouth. He also wore a black suit but a white fedora as well. The two body guards on either side of the man with the cigar escorted him quickly into the main entrance of the hotel. After they disappeared into the interior of the building, the limousine drove away to a parking space behind the hotel. The young driver locked the car and walked around the front to enter the hotel. His name was Landino Ferrini. A few years earlier he had come to Chicago at the behest of his uncle from Angri, Italy to join the Capone gang.

He took a seat in a chair in view of the elevator, which soon arrived on the lobby level. The door opened. The uniformed middle aged black operator stepped out and greeted the young driver, "Good afternoon, sir."

"Yeah, hello. . . Come on, Jeremiah, you know I'm Landi."

"Right, but I'm so used to giving every man a *Sir*. Anyway what's up with you, man?"

Landi looked around the lobby furtively and when he determined none of the mob goons were around he replied under his breath. "I gotta drive the big man up to Wisconsin as soon as he comes down. . . I spent all morning getting the 'hearse' ready for the Big man's procession up north."

"That's good you're goin' up north where it'll be cool. It's been nothing but hot here lately. Should be real cool up in the north woods. But what do you mean – 'hearse'?"

"Because when Big Al shows up it's 'curtains' for anybody that crosses him. . . But it'll be a bore up there for me. Nobody like you to talk to. Just hang around while 'ol Scarface' has fun at night and big meetings during the afternoons. . .He'll sleep in 'til noon up there just like here."

The elevator buzzer rang. Jeremiah stepped back into the elevator car and closed the door.

Landi had a premonition and so got up and stood at attention in case it was his boss who was coming down. The door opened and one of the body guards came out and went over to the desk. The Desk clerk tapped the button to ring for a bellman. Two uniformed bellhops showed up and followed the man in black to the elevator. The man nudged Landi, "Have the car ready in front."

Jeremiah gave a 'good-bye' to Landi before he closed the door. "See you when you get back to town."

"Maybe! Bye," Landi replied as he hurried out the main entrance to bring the car around. He was ready when the bellmen came out with the baggage. When these were loaded, Landi knew to drive around to a rear entrance where the bodyguards and Big Al climbed into the car. He then sped away up Michigan Avenue bound for northern Wisconsin.

Wonder what he meant by 'maybe' Jeremiah pondered as he saw the black Cadillac move off.

Landi made his way up through the city taking Milwaukee Avenue to get to the highway up to Wisconsin. He drove past a familiar block in which his memory had been seared with a tragic and sordid experience which would continue to give him deeply troubling dreams. Dreams in which he saw the bodies of a man and woman splayed across a bloody sidewalk.

CHAPTER 2

Illinois City, Montana —1902 and in the years following

The cries of a newborn infant could be heard coming from one of the bedrooms upstairs in the Mayor's Mansion, as it had come to be called. It was a clear morning in late May of 1902 when word spread throughout the town that Clara Hudson had given birth to her first child. It was the height of lilac season, which Hubert and Clara celebrated by naming their first child Lilacia.

Pampered by Mayor Hudson and his wife, Clara, Lilacia would grow to be a beautiful maiden who would affectionately be called Laci. Married in her early twenties. Within a few years she would be widowed when a tragic accident one morning took the life of her husband Howard Olsen. After that she moved back into her childhood room in the upper story of the Mayor's House.Still as beautiful as the day of her wedding, Laci's life was sadly muted by the fateful ending of hope for a long life of joy and happiness with Howard.

Soon after Howard's death, Hubert Hudson was afflicted with a serious stroke rendering him bed-ridden. Laci had moved home where she and Clara would live like sisters now in the Mayor's Mansion, helping each other in the care of Laci's father, Clara's husband, who lay helpless. While the stroke restricted his ability to use his arms or legs, he remained lucid, able to hear but to speak only awkwardly.

Clara and Laci were in need of additional help, and so it was fortuitous that Laci accidentlay came across such a person. Laci had gone down to the local mercantile for a few groceries when a young woman who had obviously just gotten off the train wandered into the store and was greeted by the clerk. "Howdy, ma'am. What can I do for you?"

"I'm looking for work."

Laci noticed that there was something furtive in her response. She carried a small cheap looking suit case. Her clothes seemed out of place—more like what one would find in an eastern city.

The storekeeper asked. "What kind of work are you seeking?"

"Oh, most anything. I'm down to my last few dollars."

"Well, what sort of work have you done?"

Laci saw that the young woman seemed embarrassed when she replied, "I guess you'd call it housework—also I worked at a soda fountain and cafe."

When Laci heard the woman's response, she offered."My mother needs some help now that my father is bedridden. She might be interested in you. What is your name and how can she reach you, may I ask?"

"My name is Eleanor Ann Helm. But I just got off the train and don't have a place to stay." Her embarrassment seemed to be tinged with pleading now, which led Laci to offer to this stranger, "You could come home with me now, and if Mother thinks you might be able to help, perhaps we can find you a room."

"Oh, that would be wonderful. . . if she will have me."

With that the two women left the store and began their walk to Laci's house. Laci worried the whole time that she had held out a false hope to this stranger and that her mother would not accept the young woman.

She needn't have worried. The stranger was immediately put to work and Laci was given the task of fixing up an empty attic room for Eleanor Helm. However, getting acquainted with the new household helper was another matter. She preferred taking her meals in the kitchen, and sometimes in her room rather than to eat with Laci and her mother. Whenever she was asked about her personal history, she immediately clammed up and said little.

As a result of Mr. Hudson's stroke, the work of the mines and the processing plant had come under the direction of Clara Hudson. Now that the new girl had come to work in the house, Clara would have much more time to devote to the family business. This arrangement proved failry effective for the first few years after Hubert's stroke while Hubert was still able to give directions from his bed. But this lasted only so long.

One day while seated at her father's bedside Laci watched a strange man in a black suit and tweed cap carrying a suit case as he walked past and stepped up onto the porch of Morettis' house next door. She noticed that when he knocked on the front door he wasn't immediately invited in. After a certain amount of conversation he was let in.

During this entrance drama next door, Eleanor was quietly sweeping the porch of the Hudson house. When she saw the man in the black suit walk up to the door, she immediately turned away and began sweeping in a far corner of the porch. *Of all things* she thought *he looks strangely familiar. Could he be someone I might have seen in Chicago?*

CHAPTER 3

Mercer, Wisconsin in the 1920s

The house faced the lake shore and was totally isolated from the public road behind it. It was a very dark summer night when one of the doors of the garage behind the house was stealthily opened. A black Cadillac four-door sedan was secretly pushed by two men out of the garage and down the drive way far enough from the house not to be seen from it. It was rolled up to the crest of a slight hill leading to the entrance to the compound. One of the two pushers, a young man, got into the driver's seat and very quietly closed his door and signaled to the second person who was poised, ready to give the car a final push so that it began to roll down the hill through a pine forest. The car moved soundlessly with neither its headlights on nor its engine running. When it emerged from the forest and coasted onto the paved road, the young driver took a single key from his billfold and inserted it into the ignition switch. He turned the key and pressed his right foot on a round starter pedal. The engine came to life and the car headed south as fast as the shiny black sedan could go.

Six hours later the sun was just rising over the horizon behind him as he drove into Portage, Wisconsin. He found a used car lot, and parked the black Cadillac in a row of automobiles for sale. He removed his Illinois license plates and everything in the car which might reveal his identity. He stuffed these things into his small leather valise and walked to the Northern Pacific Railroad station. He went into the men's room, re-brushed his hair into a different style, took a neck tie out of his suit case and put in on. Next he slipped on a black suit coat and horn rimmed glasses. A tweed cap completed his image change. At the ticket window the agent asked "Where to?"

"Missoula, Montana, sir."

"Round-trip?"

"No. One way."

The agent told him the price. The young man paid in cash. The agent handed him the required ticket. The young man took a seat among a small group of people waiting for the westbound passenger train. He read a newspaper shielding his face from view. The train finally arrived and he stood up, looked around furtively and went out onto the platform, mounted the step onto one of the coaches and found a seat alone. He immediately took out his newspaper again while other passengers were passing by. Soon he heard the *All aboard* over the pulsing sound of the steam engine. Then slowly the train began to roll forward. He put away his paper and seemed to relax, but he tensed up when the conductor came by to punch his ticket.

Landino felt his nerves loosen as the train soon reached its normal speed a few miles into the countryside northwest of Portage. Seated alone and looking out his window, Landino Ferrini began to take stock of his situation. The green pasturelands dotted with black and white dairy cows reminded him of is native Italy. He missed his home and his family. He wished his domineering uncle had never talked him into coming with him to America. And then to Chicago. At first Landi had been impressed with Big Al, his uncle's boss, and later his boss, for whom he had become a chauffeur. But not anymore. He had shaken off the iron grip of Big Al. *Or have I?*

A fateful image had come to him in a dream one night not long ago. He had felt in his dream like a tiny insect caught in a huge web, encompassing everything in sight. Big Al was the spider who had spun the web and now had complete control over everything caught in it. It was one of those dreams in which one urgently wants to get somewhere but cannot seem to make it. In the morning he knew he had been captured in the web of insidious organized crime which had spread its malicious web over all of the metropolitan area of Chicago—and beyond.

As a chauffeur, Landino had not been among the major players in this violent underground game, yet he could gather information about the activities of the Mob as he listened from around the edges. He learned that the Capone organization had gained control over a massive manufacture and distribution of illegal booze during this ill-fated era of nationwide Prohibition. In addition, the "Outfit," as it was known, controlled gambling, prostitution, bootlegging, dog-racing and other illegal activities in the city of Chicago and in many of its suburbs, such as Cicero and Melrose Park, to name a few. The syndicate's web maintained vicious control over its challengers through many forms of extortion and intimidation including violence and murder. In Ferrini's five years he had seen the streets of the city strewn with enemies of the Capone mob gunned down by its hit men.

He had become sick of it. He then had determined to escape the spider's deathly web. His determination was given direction when a letter came to him from a girl he had known in his home town in Italy.

> *Dear Landino,*
>
> *Father tells me that you have moved to America and live in Chicago. I also have come to America, and now live in Illinois City, Montana. However it is lonely here, for there are no other families from our country living here. It would be wonderful to see you again and better yet if you could move here. There are still some jobs here for young men in the gold mines nearby.*
>
> *I hope I can hear from you soon.*
>
> *Arrivederci,*
> *Loreto*

Landi read and re-read Loreto's letter. She brought back to him a warm feeling which he'd not felt since coming to America. He remembered how he and Loreto had been good friends as children, and how when they had gotten a bit older he had felt a growing attraction to her. Before anything could develop between them her family had left for the U.S. He really had not known how she felt toward him. But, now, her letter gave him a sliver of hope that perhaps she felt something for him

Her letter had a way of firming up his intention to leave the Mob and Chicago and to forsake that sordid life behind him. More and more, as he thought about her letter, he became determined to see Loreto again. Landi was afraid to write very much to his old acquaintance, but he finally slipped a short note to her by return mail.

Dear Loreto,

I was very happy to hear from you and surprised. Someday I will try to come and see you.

Addio,
Landino

PS. By the way, since I am in America I am changing my name to an American name. Call me Harland now, Harland Ferris.

Now Landino Ferrini was free and he was riding into the far west, out of the reaches of Big Al's tentacles, he believed. He was on his way to Illinois City, Montana. He would see Loreto Moretti. . . and to start a new life. . . perhaps with Loreto. He would be on the train overnight before arriving in Missoula the next day. Then he was told that train on a spur line to Illinois City would carry him the rest of the way.

It was mid-morning the next day when young Ferrini sat in the station in Missoula waiting for the train to Illinois City. After a short train ride, in early afternoon he found himself in a strange new world walking down a dirt street until he came to a wooden stairway built against an earthen cliff. He mounted these stairs. Once at the top he came to the house he was looking for. He mounted the steps to the front porch and went forward to ring the door bell. Eleanor Helm, the maid next door noticed him from her porch.

Mercer, Wisconsin

It was eight o'clock in the morning back in Mercer. Two men were in the dining room of the big house having breakfast. The man at the head of the table asked, "Where's Ferrini this morning?"

"Dunno, Boss." the other answered.

"I want him to take me into town in a half an hour," The boss explained.

"He's probably out in the garage. I'll check."

In a few minutes he returned. "No trace of Ferrini. What's more, the Cadillac is gone."

"Find him!"

Just then a car was heard driving up the almost hidden lane to the cabin.

"There he is, Boss."

But it was another man coming through the back door with an urgent message. "Boss, you gotta get back to town. There's trouble brewing."

"Sit down and tell me about it."

The three men sat at the table while the newcomer explained.

In minutes all thee men piled into the Lincoln sedan which had just arrived, and they headed for Chicago.

"What about the kid, Al?"

"Forget him. He didn't know anything. He's replaceable."

"I'll keep him on the list. We may want to take care of him. Right, Boss?"

"Right."

CHAPTER 4

Illinois City, Montana

The stranger at the door had been talking with a house maid when a booming voice came from within the house. "Landino Ferrini, welcome to The Moretti House. Please come in. You have come a long way, have you not?"

"Yes sir, all the way from Chicago," Landi said as he entered the hallway.

"From Italy before that, no?"

"Yes."

"Come into my parlor." Turning to the maid, he said, "Please bring us some tea, Dolores."

The two men were seated and Pietro Moretti leaned forward to look at Landino. "So tell me about yourself."

Having long anticipated this question, Landi answered in general terms. "I came to this country about five years ago and went to Chicago at my 'uncle's' suggestion. I was given a job as the chauffeur for one of the bosses in his company. I have been doing that ever since."

"Ah, yes. I remember your 'uncle' Ralph. He is in Chicago, then?"

"Yes."

Moretti hesitated and then went ahead with his next question. "What business is he in?"

"He has a business that delivers things around the city. A trucking company."

"I see...what sort of things?"

"I really don't know. He doesn't tell me much."

"The man you drive for. . . he's in the business too?"

"That, plus a lot of other stuff."

"He gave you some time off, did he?"

"My boss is on vacation right now—up in Wisconsin."

"And he doesn't need you up there?"

Landi hesitated. "Well, sir. I just quit him after driving him up to his summer house in the north woods. And I thought I'd just come out here to Montana and try something else."

"Oh?"

"Loreto wrote me and told me that there might be work in the mines." Landi thought then to ask Moretti, "Are you in the mining business?"

"No. I have a mercantile store and a café down on Main Street. Mines are slowing down"

There was a knock on the door and Landi looked startled with fear in his eyes.

"Come in, Dolores."

The door opened and the maid came in. "Here is your tea, sir."

Landi looked relieved.

"And, Dolores, would you get the guest room ready for our visitor?"

"Of course."

While the two drank their tea, his host told Landi about the town and other things about the area. "As you can see, most of Illinois City is down the hill from here. Our Mercantile and café are down on Main Street. We and the Hudsons are the only places up here. Hudson owns the mines. Hudson's grandfather came from Illinois and found gold here and started the town. Named it after his home state."

At the mention of Illinois, the younger man became hot and sweaty. The tea he'd been drinking and the questioning had been making him anxious as well.

"You look flushed, Landino. You have had a long trip. Why don't go up to your room and refresh yourself before dinner, which is at 7. And I should say that Mrs. Moretti has been quite ill lately and is in her bed upstairs. That is where my daughter is, but I am quite sure that Loreto will be down for supper." With that he arose and ushered Landi to the stairs, where Dolores took him up to his room.

Once in his upstairs guest room and alone, Landi relaxed and took stock of all that had happened to him in the last couple of days. Only two days ago he had escaped the powerful, yet seductive grasp of Big Al, his "uncle" Ralph's brother. Ever since arriving in New York, Ralph had taken over his life and directed him each step of the way. Beyond that, the syndicate itself had determined what he would do. Where he lived, whom he talked to, where he could not go, and in every way how he lived and what he was commanded to do. That he had been pressed into service as Big Al's driver was in many ways a relief. He could have been sent out onto the street, armed and ready to kill, as many of the others had been hired to do. But the other side of it was that being the boss's driver allowed him to hear things and see things which made him hot—he would always be closely watched to see that he didn't squeal. So even though he had escaped, he was terrified that they would make every effort to find him and silence him. Here, far away in Montana, he was free. . . but not free.

He knew, however, what the Capone outfit was able to do to find guys they wanted to "take care of," especially those who too much! As Landino thought about the ability of the mob to find him, he realized that he needed to level with Pietro and make sure that his real name would no longer be used.

He stepped over to his window which looked toward the house next door, where he saw someone on the porch sweeping. When she twisted toward him, the hairs on the back of his neck bristled when he thought he recognized her. But he wasn't too sure. She resembled someone he had seen briefly when he had driven "Scarface Al" out to the west side of Chicago. The sight of anyone from his past life in Chicago was bound to cast a shroud of fear over Landi. Who she was he could not remember.

A little before seven Landino went downstairs and was again welcomed by Mr. Moretti. "Come in to supper, Landino. Dolores is upstairs with Mrs. Moretti and so Loreto will be down to supper with us."

"Ah. . . sir. . . I have something I need to tell you before I meet anyone else."

"What is it, Landi?"

"I have made the decision to use an American name instead of my Italian name. . . to sort of get along better. So could you call me Harland, Harland Ferris, especially when you introduce me to anybody?"

"Well, I suppose we could, but do you really need to do that?"

Landi showed himself to be extremely wrought up by this request when he answered. "Mr. Moreti, my life depends upon this change."

"Oh?"

"I can't tell you right now. It's a long story. But I will someday."

"If you say so. . .Harland."

"Thank you, sir."

Just then Loreto came down the stairs to join her father. When she saw Landi she exclaimed."Landino, you're here!

He father cut in. "Landino would like to be called Harland now that he's in America."

"Oh, sorry, Harland, I mean. I remember that you told me this in your letter."

"Loreto!" he said, and then he fell silent. He was tongue tied, filled with embarrassment and fear.

Mr. Moretti stepped into the breach and said. "Now, you two, you must have more to say than that. You were pals back home when you were little."

Loreto announced. "Ever since you wrote me back, I have been hoping you would come."

"I've wanted to come to see you but I couldn't find the chance to get away to see you."

"You mean you were busy with a job?"

"That, but there was more to it. Sometime I may tell you."

"Sounds mysterious."

At that, he changed the subject. "Tell me about yourself, Etti."

She bowed her face briefly in an embarrassed expression. "Well, since I wrote you I have decided to go back home to Naples."

"Really?"

"As soon as mama gets better I will go. There is just nothing here for me. And back in Italy I have friends and I can work in the family olive groves. I'll have my life back again."

Loreto's father re-entered the room to announce dinner.

"Let's sit down to eat our supper," Mr. Moretti directed.

"Yes, Papa," Loreto said, as all three sat down and Pietro and his daughter made the sign of the cross after being seated.

Moretti turned to Loreto and said, "Harland, here wants to stay around and find work. What do you think of that, Etti?"

"Wonderful, Papa." She turned to her friend, "In the mines, do you suppose?"

"Well, I guess that's where the work has been in the past, but not much anymore." He seemed to be deep in thought before making a suggestion. "But I have another idea, Harland. I need some help at the mercantile. Would you like to work for me?"

"Yes, sir, if you'd have me?'

"I can't pay you what they would have paid in the mines in the good old days. The price of gold has gone down, you know. Nor can I pay what probably you got in Chicago. By the way how much did your boss pay you?"

He flushed at this question and was evasive. "That doesn't matter, sir. Whatever you offer is fine. Just glad to get a job and to be able to stay here. . . as far from Chicago as I can get," he said almost under his breath.

"Let's see. You said you drove for your boss. I could use a man to drive our truck to town for supplies. I usually do this but with the wife so ill I hate to be gone that long at a time. Missoula is quite a ways."

"I could do that, sir. And whatever else you want me to do."

"Well, that settles it, boy. You'll start in the morning. Now I want you and Etti to go have some time to get reacquainted. So why don't you two go out on the porch while I take care of things upstairs and Dolores can clean up here."

Etti was the first to speak after both had taken chairs on the porch. "I'm glad that you have come to Montana. It has been very lonely for me here with no other people my age anymore."

"I'm glad I'm here too. And it is good to see you . . ." He was tongue-tied and didn't know how to continue his train of thought. He was disappointed when she didn't comment further about his coming, but returned to what she had said about feeling lonely.

"Recently when the people next door hired a maid, who seems to be about my age, I thought perhaps we could become friends"

"Oh?" Landi expressed interest. "I did see someone on the porch from the window upstairs. Do you know anything about her, where she came from. Or who she is?"

"No, she keeps to herself. Not very friendly."

"That's too bad. . . . for you, I mean."

"I did hear that she came from the East. Up until lately, I at least saw people when I worked at the mercantile for Papa. But when Mama got so sick I have been here in the house with her most of the time since.

I'm glad you have come to visit. That will give me someone to talk to. And you will be a big help to papa, I'm sure. Tell me about yourself, Landi. . . Oh, I mean Harland."

He replied somewhat reluctantly, "I have been in Chicago since coming to the States. My 'uncle' Ralph got me a job working for his brother in the company he manages."

"Your uncle Ralph?"

"He really isn't my uncle, but his family and ours back in Italy were very close and so when I was little, Ralph sort of adopted me, so to speak." He paused. "He's the one who talked me into coming to the U. S. and to Chicago. That's about it."

"What sort of business was your uncle in?"

"Lot's of stuff around the city. A lot of trucking of things around the city and beyond." Landi was evasive, but Etti's reaction prompted him to say a little more. "I was the low man on the totem pole. They didn't tell me much. . . so I just did my job and didn't ask questions."

"What was your job?"

"I was a driver."

"Your drove a truck?"

"No. A car for the boss. . . wherever he wanted to go. . . That's how come I was in Wisconsin. Big Al-- my boss, I mean-- had a summer place up there."

"So, you'll not be going back?"

"No, I quit and came out here after I thought about your letter."

"Good, I'm glad."

"How soon do you plan to go back to the old country?"

"It all depends upon Mama's condition. If she improves enough to be on her own, then I would feel free to leave. And if. . . God forbid. . . She doesn't make it, then after a time I would leave."

"Wouldn't your father need you at that point?"

"He thinks it would be best for me to go back, since he is convinced that Illinois City is about to close down."

"Really?"

"He says the mines are shutting down. And when they are gone there is nothing left here." Then she added, "But for the time being, I think he really needs you to help him."

"Well, I guess I'll be ok. It will be good to have a little time to get re-acquainted."

She hesitated and then told her friend. "But I need to be honest with you. Armando—you remember him . . . ."

"Yes, I do." Landi felt that he would not like what she was starting to say.

"Armando has been corresponding with me and we want to re-connect after all these years."

Landino could not help but feel a disappointment. "I'm sorry."

"I know."

CHAPTER 5

After breakfast, Pietro addressed Harland, "Come with me and I will take you to the mercantile and get you started. Then this evening we will work out your sleeping arrangements."

"Thank you, sir."

The two walked down to the store and café, where Moretti showed Harland around his establishments. The small café was included in the mercantile. Then they went behind the store and Moretti started up the truck, and had his new employee get in and see if he could drive it. "This is my Chevy one ton utility truck," he said proudly. "Think you can drive it? It's a 1926 three speed."

"Yes, sir. The boss back in Chicago had some like it."

"I want you to meet the train when it comes in with supplies for us. It comes twice a week. This morning, in fact. Around nine o'clock." Then when you return there will be a number of jobs for you, mostly stocking shelves and that sort of thing." He then added. "And the cook will have something for your lunch and supper. Then on some days I'll have you pick up some things in Missoula."

"Yes, sir. I will be glad to do whatever you want me to."

Landi found driving Pietro's truck easy for him. He met the train at nine and picked up a load of supplies marked for the mercantile and the café. He spent the rest of the day on various tasks under Pietro's direction.

When Landi returned to the Moretti house after his supper in the café, Dolores met him on the porch as he mounted the stairs. "I have a room ready for you out back in the loft of the carriage house. Come with me. I've already taken your things up there."

He followed her around the back of the house and up the outside stairs of the carriage house and into the loft where he found a bed and dresser, a wardrobe and a small table. "This is going to be quite nice for me, Dolores. Thank you for getting it ready for me."

"That's good. I hope you are going to like it here in Illinois City."

"I think I will. Just glad to get out of Chicago."

"Oh, you're from Illinois, too. My husband and I came here from Galena, Illinois. He came to work in the mines, but we weren't here long before he was killed in a mining accident.

"I'm sorry, Dolores."

"It was then that I had to find a job, so Mrs. Moretti took me on as a maid."

Harland felt a certain kinship to this woman who was possibly twenty years his senior. He replied warmly." Have they been good to you here, Dolores?

"Yes, they are good people." She was uncomfortable with this more personal conversation. "Let me show you what you can use in the yard. She directed him to a water pump and out- house beyond the carriage house for his use. "Let me know if I can get you anything else you need" she offered before returning to the big house.

Landino, alias Harland, lay down on the bed, tired after a days work. But happy with his new name and his new life in the mountains of Montana far away from Mercer, Wisconsin, and from Chicago. *Now, maybe I can shake loose of the awful grip of the mob.* As he thought about the ability of the mob to find him, he realized that if he could just get his name change set in everyone's mind he would have a chance, even if they showed up in Illinois City looking for him.

As time went on Harland fell into a comfortable routine of working two mornings in the week in the truck and the rest of his time in the mercantile. Sometimes he was asked to fill in at the café. He enjoyed his work and the new acquaintances in his life. He had less to do with Loreto than he had anticipated because of her constant vigil at her mother's side. On the other hand he enjoyed his solitude in his evening hours. But, he did feel a bit lonely. Back in Chicago there was always a bunch of the men from the Mob around. He didn't have time to be lonely. . . but yet, he had had no contact with people his own age, especially girls. *Not any different here. . except. . . .*He had occasionally spotted the young maid next door. She seemed somewhat attractive.

Slender, pretty blond hair bobbed short. She always seemed fearful and furtive in her movements about the house and yard. He had never been able to see her face very clearly. She was always wrapped in a coat of some kind.

The Moretti family and the Hudson family appeared to be quite distant from each other. However he did see Dolores talking with the maid next door once in a while. This interested Harland, because he continued to have the uneasy feeling that he had seen her before somewhere. And when he thought about it, that could really only mean Chicago. He wanted nothing to do with any aspect of his Chicago past. But yet the mystery persisted, and sooner or later he would have to find out about her. He would ask Dolores sometime about the woman.

The occasion arose when Harland found Dolores relaxing on a chair outside the back door. He went up to her. "Hello, Dolores. How's things with you today?"

"Oh fine. Just taking a rest for a spell."

"Mind if I sit down on this other chair?"

"Go ahead."

When he was seated he tried to sound casual when he asked, "You're friends with the maid next door?"

"Yeah, we talk once in a while. But she's very quiet"

"What do you know about her?"

"Nothing much, really."

"What's her name?

"Eleanor."

"I see." Harland was quiet for a while and then asked. "Where's she come from?"

"I believe she said some place in Illinois. . . Cicero, I think it was."

Harland gave a knowing look. "What'd she do back there? Do you know?"

"I asked her. She wouldn't say. Just clammed up"

"Is that all?"

"Yeah. . . but I don't know. There's something about her that bothers me." She paused while she seemed to think. "She seems to be afraid of something. . . and there is a sadness about her."

Harland hesitated and then said, "I'd like to meet her."

"Why?" Then Dolores looked sheepish, "I guess that's a dumb question."

"No. The reason is that I think I've seen her before, and I'd just like to see if I have."

Dolores responded to Harland's wish. "I'll see if I can arrange that. OK?"

"Thanks." Harland returned to the carriage house and went up to his room, thinking about what Dolores had told him of Eleanor. *So, she's from Cicero. Big Al has a lot going on in Cicero. I wonder. . . How'd she get here?. . . Maybe that's why she appears sad and clams up. . . .*

CHAPTER 6

It took Harland a couple of months to let loose of his Chicago past and to begin to relax, free of fear. Eventually he was coming to feel at home in Illinois City, and in the surrounding mountains. However he was often haunted with recurring dreams of his Chicago experiences. Especially, often the drive-by shooting came to him in his dreams, usually waking him up in a sweat.

During his off hours he found himself more and more drawn to the mountains and their natural wild beauty. He had long since shed his Chicago clothing, the black suit, white shirt and black cap. He'd gotten some woolen trousers and flannel shirts at the mercantile, which were much more practical, especially for his treks out into the nearby mountains. More important, he now felt that he fit in with the locals. He was beginning to accept himself as "Harland." "Landi" was starting to sound alien to him.

One Sunday morning after Pietro and Loreto went to mass while Dolores stayed home to care for Mrs. Moretti, Harland slipped out of the carriage house and headed up the trail behind it into the woods. He mounted a steady climb until he emerged from the pine forest into an open meadow filled with bright sunlight illuminating the native grasses. He found a fallen log on which to rest. To the southwest, the Garnet Range formed a panoramic backdrop.

As he soaked up the beauty of this isolated glen, his mind went into reverse. *Six months ago, about now, I would be kneeling during mass in Assumption Parish Church in the heart of Chicago. A huge church compared to our little church in Italy. Chicago was a massive city in every way. Crowds—always crowds. Trucks and cars on the streets day and night. I was always surrounded by three or four story buildings. Couldn't see much sky. I felt trapped.* He looked up from his gaze backward in time and saw the mountains in the distance and a sea of tree tops in the foreground. Instead of the indistinguishable noises of the busy streets he heard the chirping of birds and the buzz of insects in midst of quiet solitude. Harland could hardly comprehend what a difference had come into his life. *A good difference.* He thought. Not only the scenery and the sounds, but he felt that the heavy shackle of evil was being lifted from his life, after escaping the clutch of the "outfit."

He had been refusing to go to mass since coming to Illinois City. There had been something dishonest about going to mass at Assumption parish that deepened his feeling of being shackled by evil. He'd often seen Al Capone and members of the "outfit" sitting in the pews near him on Sunday mornings. It didn't seem right to him, after he had heard his boss and his pals discuss their devious and violent plans during the week. As Big Al's driver he would overhear things. In fact, over time Harland heard more than he could stomach, sometimes giving him a sick feeling. The innocence of his childhood in Italy had been stolen by the men of the Mob who had taken over his young life. As he thought about it now, it had been his growing feeling of sin and evil which had made him think about escaping.

The incident which pushed him all the way to take steps to escape occurred shortly before they were to go up to Mercer, Wisconsin to Big Al's hide-away.

One morning when Landi reported for work, Frank "the enforcer" Nitti summoned him to his office. "Yes sir."

"Kid, I need you to drive for us this afternoon. My drive-by driver is sick and we have a bit of business to take care of this afternoon."

With that, Harland had been pressed into the despicable job of driving the car in which two of Nitto's hit men would be in the back seat behind darkened glass. As he understood it, Big Al's outfit needed to take out one of the leaders of a rival organization in order to gain control over the North Side. So it became Landino's job to drive the car by a café on Milwaukee Avenue at an appointed time with two of Nitto's hit men in the back seat, poised with sawed-off shot guns ready to fire when they passed by their chosen victim.

Landi drove the prescribed route and when they passed by a couple walking on the side-walk, the Mob's two men rolled down the side window, took aim and fired. As a horrible result, a prominent leader of a competing mob and his wife lay dead on the cement outside the cafe. Landi sped away and quickly disappeared into an anonymous stream of traffic on busy Milwaukee Avenue before the double murder was discovered.

Harland had not been hardened to this act of violence. Afterwards he was deeply repulsed by the killing he had been involved in. The awful sound of the gunfire echoed and re-echoed in his ears for the rest of the day and into the night. He had been instrumental in the killing of not only the rival gangster, but of his innocent wife as well. Who knew, but what there might have been children orphaned by his action that day. Landi could not rid himself of the bloody image he had seen on the sidewalk. The next morning, after a sleepless night, he resolved to find a way to throw off the shackles of the syndicate and to escape to become anonymous. He wanted no more of this life in the mob. It could only get worse, he knew.

It was soon after that excruciating incident that Landino found his escape route from Big Al's cabin the north woods at Mercer, Wisconsin.

Now, at last he was free and hidden away in the isolated woods of Montana. No longer an errand boy for the Mob and now a legitimate truck driver for Moretti's Mercantile. No longer Landino Ferrini of the criminal underbelly of Chicago, but Harland Ferris of Illinois City, Montana!

As he sat amid the quiet grandeur of the mountain meadow, Harland was beginning to feel cleansed as the bright sun warmed his body. While he had been taught that going to confession and then receiving communion from the priest would cleanse his sin, Big Al's close association with the church had spoiled the effectiveness of the sacraments of the church for Harland. Now he was trying to find absolution on his own in the quiet solitude of nature.

Not long after Harland began his hike up the hill, the housemaid from the Mayor's Mansion next door began a walk up the same trail. She also had been given some free time on this Sunday morning. As she slowly made her way along the trail, she thought about her situation. Glad for the work and especially relieved to be away from Chicago, she nevertheless remained fearful of being discovered for what her former life had been. In fact she suspected that somehow word had followed her. She was afraid that her employer assumed the worst and was treating her accordingly. Laci also had remained aloof. The result of this, she realized that she felt totally isolated from any friendly human contact. And she admitted to herself that she was lonely.

She told herself over and over again that she herself had not "fallen." It was just that when she saw what other girls her own age were forced to do upstairs she felt dirtied by it and somehow contaminated, as though she had sinned. And, obviously she thought, it showed. Others must know. And so being alone as she walked on a path in the forest was a great relief to Eleanor. Away from the thoughts and gazes of others.

As the trail bent slightly to the left, she found an opening between the trees which revealed a vista looking downward upon the valley below. In the distance she could see a farmhouse surrounded by crop land. Momentarily, bittersweet thoughts of her family home in Iowa welled up in her consciousness. *Oh, why did I ever leave? It was a good life. Back on the farm when I was little, then when we moved to town. My family loved me. How I miss our house. It was so good to come home to my room and to enjoy family times in the living room and meals in the dining room. Father called it "The house on Avenue I." And in the summer I loved walking in the back yard, under the grape arbor and picking bunches of those dark blue Concord grapes. I had school friends nearby. They loved to come over to my yard and we'd play together when we were little. . . Then after graduation I thought I could be happy with a job at Schaeffer's. . . but it was too dull, I thought. . . So then I decided I had to leave—to start an exciting new life—I thought.*

She remembered that day in town when she boarded the bus for Chicago. Her mother had cried. Her little sister, Emily, had clung to her skirt. Her father seemed so awkward and stiff. *And I was so excited. I was going to get such a good job and make money and have a classy apartment. I thought about how I would meet a young man and how we might fall in love.* Tears came to her eyes. *And all I got was into that dump on Madison Street—that den of iniquity.*

She could no longer look at farm houses in the distance. They reminded her of her early days in Iowa. Her sight was filled with tears. Her thoughts were too painful. She was ashamed ever to return to her family. She resumed her walk.

Harland jumped when he heard a sudden snapping of a branch followed by footsteps. He sat very still as he watched a figure emerge from the woods along the path and enter the sunlight of the meadow. It was a woman. He recognized her. She was the maid from the house next door to Morettis. He saw her freeze when she saw him. She started to turn around and to go back the way she had come. Harland called with as gentle a voice as he could muster, "Don't run away. I won't hurt you."

She stopped and turned back to him. He continued, "Don't be afraid, you can pass me and get ahead. I'm just sort of resting here for a while."

She hesitated and then relaxed a little. "I'm not going anywhere either."

"Sit down if you want to. It is so beautiful and peaceful here."

She seemed to think about that and then said,"I guess I will." She sat down on the same log some distance away from Harland. She sat erect as if she were ready to jump up and run if anything should frighten her. He sensed this and did not say anything for a while until he felt that she might have become a bit more at ease.

"My name's Harland, I'm in the carriage house next to where you are."

"Yes, I live in the attic of the Mayor's house. I work there."

"What's your name, may I ask?"

"Eleanor Ann."

They were both quiet for a few minutes as each of them looked out to the mountains. Then Harland asked, "Have you been there long?"

"Three or four months."

"I've just been here a few weeks."

"I know."

"You do?"

"Yes. I was on the Mayor's porch when you first came and knocked on the Moretti's door."

"Yeah, I had just gotten off the train."

"Where did you come from?

"I'd come on the train from Wisconsin to Missoula. . ." He considered letting it go at that but then added. "Before that–Chicago and before Chicago–Italy." When she did not have anything to say, he asked, "How about you? Have you always lived around here?"

"No." She appeared hesitant to reveal more of her background. Harland sensed this and didn't want to push. She struggled with herself and then told him. "My earliest days were on a farm in Iowa. Then in grade school we moved to town. . . to Ft. Madison. . . When I graduated from high school, I worked for a short while at Scheaffer Pen in Ft. Madison, but I got bored after a few months.

"So you came out here to find work?"

"No, not right away." She looked at him with a sheepish expression and then stared at the ground, rubbing her shoe back and forth in the stony dirt of the trail. Then she said, "I thought that I could find a good job in Chicago so I went there and looked for a job."

"That took some courage. Did you have a place to stay while you looked for work?"

"A friend of mine from home had a place there and she gave me a room until I found an apartment and a job."

"So then you must have found something."

"I sort of did, but it didn't last long."

"Where was your job?"

She hesitated. "Out on West Madison Street."

"Doing what?"

After a long pause, "I worked at a soda fountain. It wasn't what I expected. After a while my boss who lived in an apartment above the shop wanted me to take a job upstairs. . .to be one of her girls. . ."

Landi could guess what was upstairs above the soda fountain. . . In fact it dawned on him. *That was where I saw her—on the street when Al stopped there to talk with one of his people.* "Would that have paid more?"

Eleanor seemed very hesitant to say more. "Yeah, I guess." but then she added, "She showed me what it would be like. It was awful. I quit. . .I ran away, really. . . That's when I came here."

By that time Harland knew for sure what kind of place she had been in, and so he did not ask any more questions. "Well, I guess you are glad to have gotten here—away from Chicago."

"Yes I am." She turned the conversation to his situation. "Do you work in the mines?"

"No, I work for Mr. Moretti at the store and the café. I drive his truck on errands a lot." He turned the discussion back to her situation. "Do you like working at the Mayor's house?"

"It's a job. Better than Chicago. But I don't get along too well with Laci and her mother."

"What seems to be the trouble?" He showed concern.

"They treat me like scum. . . ever since. . . I think they found out about my Chicago experience."

"Oh? What's that got to do with it?"

"Who knows?" she became evasive and then announced, "Oh. . . well, I need to get back," and as an after-thought, "Do you always come here on Sundays?"

"No, this is my first time, but it is so nice here, I thought I'd stay here for a while to relax."

"This was a new spot for me too."

With that she got up abruptly and headed back down the hill.

On the way down the hill, Eleanor thought about Harland's questions. *He seemed genuinely interested in my welfare. It wasn't like he was nosy, or critical. Maybe I shouldn't have held back so much.* She found herself wishing she could have another chance to say more to Harland. It felt good to have someone to talk to, other than her employers who had become less than friendly.

Harland remained a little longer, thinking about what his neighbor had said.. After a while, as he got up to go down the trail the thought came to him. *I wonder if she could have been asked to be one of Jack Zuta's girls. He had a couple of places out on West Madison, I'm pretty sure. That would explain why they treat her like scum as well as how she must feel about herself.*

It was both curiosity and a vague attraction to Eleanor that made him hope that there might be other opportunities for them to meet and to get acquainted.

As Harland made his way back to his lonely quarters in the carriage house, he made up his mind to spend his Sunday afternoons exploring the area. . . and perhaps seeing Eleanor again.

On the following Sunday, Eleanor took the path on which she had met Harland. Not willing to admit it, she was nevertheless in hopes that he might be on this trail again. She rounded the familiar bend and entered the open meadow. She came to the same log where she and Harland had visited. She kept looking around to see if he was anywhere near, but she was disappointed and thought perhaps he would not come up to the same spot.

Harland had been detained with a few chores he needed to do before heading up into the woods as he had planned to do all week. Finally he began his hike, looking forward to the restful place where he had stopped the week before. As he rounded the bend and entered the clearing, he felt a thrill go though him as he saw her seated on the log. She was obviously looking around for someone. He couldn't believe it. *Could she possibly be looking for me?*

As he drew near, she smiled at him and patted the log next to her. He sat down next to her and said, "Eleanor, I didn't know you would be here."

"I enjoyed talking with you last week, so I thought I'd see if you were here this week And you are!" She blushed in embarrassment when she thought about what she had just said.

Harland didn't exactly know how to respond and said, "I'm glad I did."

They were both, in fact tongue-tied for what to each seemed like a long time. The only sound was that of birds singing in the distance and the occasional rustle of tree branches nearby.

Eleanor then spoke up. "It seemed to me that I was awfully closed mouth last week and you were genuinely interested. Most of all you didn't think ill of me for my Chicago days.

"Not at all. I know we both have some very bad memories of our time there. Stuff we want to forget. . . and now for the first time I am able to spill my feelings to someone."

"Me too."

They both were reluctant to pursue this line of thought any further at this point and so they began sharing with each other what their day to day lives were like here in Illinois City. They found that they enjoyed this kind of free and easy conversation. The time flew by and soon they realized it was time to go back to town. They got up and made their way back together.

CHAPTER 7

On one of Harland's Sunday explorations he found a wagon road which led to a cemetery surrounded by a wrought iron fence with an arched gate at the entrance. He opened the rusty squeaking gate and wandered among the grave stones, many of which were fairly recent. A good many of the death dates had been in 1918. *The flu epidemic,* he thought. The grounds and the graves were apparently under good care. However, beyond the fence the weeds had grown profusely. He would learn later that the flu epidemic of 1918 had struck Illinois City quite hard.

He was startled to see a figure of a woman kneeling outside the fence at the far end of the enclosed area. It was obvious to him that she had been weeping. He hesitated to bother a mourner, and so turned to leave. But as he turned he looked back once more to see that the person was a young woman who was now standing. It was Eleanor. Harland quickly found a larger grave stone behind which he could avoid being seen as Eleanor left the area. After she was gone he stepped outside the fence and went to the wooden marker at the grave which Eleanor had been visiting outside the fence.

A small area had been cleared beyond the cemetery to accommodate one lone grave. The crude marker had the following inscription painted in black letters: *Wilda–Known to many, friend of none. Shot and killed. R.I.P.* Not nearly as well kept as the graves inside the fence, the weeds here had almost taken over.

When Harland found his way to his favorite spot on the mountain trail. Harland wondered about the location of the grave outside the fence, and about Eleanor's relationship to the person buried in it.

He did not see her when she came through the opening into the glen they had found. As she came closer she saw that his eyes were closed, as if in prayer. His face seemed strained. His hands were folded in his lap. She crept over to the log and very quietly sat down upon it. A bit closer to Harland than the first time they had met. She sat without making a sound, wondering if she should awaken him.

A slight wisp of wind blew across both of the hikers and had the effect of causing Harland to open his eyes and to see his young neighbor sitting near him on the log. "Eleanor. How long have you been here?"

"Not long," she said, looking at him more directly now. "Did I disturb you? You look so troubled."

Before he could answer, she saw him suddenly jerk twice in succession. "What's the matter, Harland?" She was obviously concerned.

"Oh, I . . . ." He stopped to shake his head back and forth as if to remove something covering his face. "I'm sorry. I get these attacks every so often when I least expect them."

"Attacks?"

"Yeah–like hearing two gunshots."

"Oh my!" She thought for a moment. "Why gunshots? What's that about?"

He turned to her with a look of appeal. "Eleanor, it is a long and sordid story."

"That's too bad. Can you tell me about it?"

"No." He seemed to think about his abrupt answer. "Maybe sometime, later."

"That's ok, Harland. . . Are you better now?"

"Yeah, let's talk about something else."

She remembered her nostalgic view along the trail from her previous visit to this path. "Back along the trail when I look down into the valley I see a farm house which makes me think of my childhood home in Iowa, especially when we lived in the country, before we moved into town. It makes me realize that I miss Iowa. The farm and also our home in town"

"What was your home like?"

"On the farm we had milk cows, and raised hogs as well as crops, corn and some beans and grain. I helped with the chickens and geese."

"Were there others in your family?"

"I have a younger sister. We had good times at home in those days." She turned to him with the beginning of tears in her eyes. "Tell me about your home and family."

"Back in Italy I had four brothers and a sister. I was the youngest. That's why I came to America. The place couldn't support all of us."

"Was it a farm?"

"We raised olives."

"Do you miss those days?"

"I do, but I have lost track of my family. My life in Chicago cut me off from everyone I ever knew. . . It was no good there. . . no good at all . . . for man or beast."

"I know. . .Do you like it here, Harland?"

"Yes, but I'm sort of all alone in the world, you might say." Unwilling to say it out loud he thought *until you came into my life*.

"I know what you mean."

Both were pensive. Then Eleanor said quietly. "I've not had anyone to talk to like this. . .since leaving home."

Harland felt a sort of inner nudge as he saw an imploring look in Eleanor's eyes. "Yes. . . You make these Sundays when we meet special to me."

She appeared to blush when she replied, "I know what you mean."

With that, Eleanor sensed that the conversation was over and began to get up. Harland got up and took her hand and helped her up. The two walked down the trail mostly in silence still holding each other's hand. When they got close to their houses, Harland said, "It was good to talk . . . to be with you."

"Yes. Next Sunday," she said shyly, "Hudsons are having some sort of dinner for a few friends and need me to work. But the following Sunday I could."

"Fair enough. We might as well walk up there together."

The next Sunday, Harland didn't feel like going up the hill without Eleanor, so he slept in. He got up and went to the café for a bit of lunch before returning to his room. The mercantile was closed on Sundays but the café was open. The only other customer was Mort Gibson, the ticket agent and telegrapher from the Northern Pacific Railroad station in town. He was about the age of Pietro. Harland took a stool next to him at the counter.

He greeted Harland, "Hello, boy."

"Hello, Mort." Harland had come to know the man from the station when he picked up or delivered things at the depot. "Hardly any business on Sundays," the man explained.

After some idle chit chat, Mort asked Harland. "Where'd you come from before here?"

"Chicago. Did some driving, but got tired of the big city."

"That so? I always thought I'd like to see a place like that. I've never been east of Glendive."

"That's where you grew up?"

"Yeah. Eastern Montana. But I learned telegraphing in Reed Point on the N.P. From old Pat Huntley."

"Where's that?"

"A little west of Billings—the biggest city I've ever been in."

"I see."

"Anyhow, after he thought I was good enough, Huntley gets me a job on the telegraph at Bearmouth. Then the NP put me here. . ." He seemed to be deep in thought before going on. "The wife and I rented a little house down the hill on the other side the tracks. . . she died a couple of years ago. I still live in the house. But I want to move outta here. The town's dryin' up."

"Oh?"

"Yeah. The mines are beginning to shut down. Less and less ore goin' outa' here. Used to be three thousand people here. Now I'd be surprised if there's even a thousand."

"Where do you plan to go?"

"I put in for a job at the depot in Helena. But I haven't heard yet." Mort finished his coffee and got up to leave. "Gotta get back."

"Bye."

Lou, the café cook and waitress, came around the counter and sat down next to Harland. He greeted her and said, "You hear Mort? He wants to leave town."

"I know. He's not the only one." She seemed to be counting herself. "I know of five other families trying to find work somewhere else."

"I got the impression things were slowing down, but I thought just temporarily."

"No. I"m afraid they've had their boom —now the bust is a-comin'. I saw it before. Just like over ta Elkhorn. I had a café there, but by the end, I was goin' broke. So I closed up and came over here and got this job with Moretti. . ." She looked perplexed. "And I don't have any idea where I'll be next."

Just then the door opened and a family of four came in. "Here comes the St. Ignatius crowd. Mass must be over and they all can have breakfast now." She hurried back of the counter. "After them'll come the Methodists for Sunday dinner."

"While the Catholics are still here?"

"Oh, sure. They all get along fine."

"Wow. That's not true where I come from."

"I know, but here it's different. I'll tell you the reason sometime." She got up to begin serving her incoming customers.

Harland sat a while wondering what was ahead for him, if the town was going bust. And Eleanor. We were just getting acquainted. Thinking about Eleanor gave him a good feeling.

CHAPTER 8

Church Alley - Autumn 1928

Behind the street on which the hotel and the Lodge Hall were located was a narrow street more or less up against the bluff on which the Mayor's Mansion stood. It had come to be called Church Alley because both the churches in town were there. On the west end of the block stood St. Ignatius with its rectory next to it. On the east corner-- Asbury Methodist, with its parsonage was located to the west. Father Patrick O'Malley had been assigned to St. Ignatius from its founding. Everybody assumed this would be his last parish, for he was in his 70's. In contrast, Pastor Dale Parker was beginning his ministry at Asbury. Most everyone in town knew that the good relations between the two church began, not with some theological discussion out of which came some agreement. No, it was domestic. Asbury didn't pay very well and so Adeline Parker had needed to find some work to help with the Parker budget. Miss Sadie, the good Catholic parishioner who cooked and kept house for Fr. O'Malley died not long after the Parkers arrived in town. Adeline found this to be an excellent opportunity and was quickly hired by the priest down the block. The talk in town was that Father hadn't wanted to miss a meal after losing Miss Sadie, who had been five years older than her employer, and so was ready to retire before her boss. However, there was other talk around town, mostly in the Methodist congregation which didn't see the matter so kindly. They were, however unable or unwilling to remedy the situation with a bit more pay for their young preacher. The more Christian response to all this was that the two clergymen became good friends.. And to a certain extent the parishioners in the two churches followed suit, much to the surprise of later additions to Illinois City like Harland Ferris.

On the next Sunday when Eleanor met Harland as he came down from the loft in the carriage house she suggested, "Let's go to church first, Harland."

"OK, but not to the Catholic Church."

"Don't worry, I'm Methodist."

They made their way down the hill and along the alley to Asbury Church.

At the café after church, the two new friends each had a bowl of soup and a slice of bread while they talked over their experience in church that morning. Eleanor was very quiet. Harland began.

"That was the first time I ever went to a Protestant church. The priests never let us do that."

"How'd you like it?"

"It was alright–a bit strange to me."

"I was quite moved by something Pastor Parker said at the end of his sermon."

"What was that?"

"He said: *No matter what you've done or where you have spent your days and nights, the Lord wants you. He wants to make you clean again.*" She choked up as she repeated her pastor's words.

Harland was silent while she daubed her eyes with her handkerchief. "Yeah, I heard that too, but I guess it didn't sink in." He added almost to himself, "it certainly wasn't what the sisters used to say."

Eleanor recovered. "Well it sank in to me. He made me think about some of the stuff that went on in Chicago, the things I wanted to get away from."

"Me too. Now that you mention it."

She looked at hm with a question.

He quietly stated, "Like the shots which come back to me in those scary attacks I get."

"Oh!" She looked at him with a new softness. "Like shots you heard in the distance in Chicago?"

"No. Not in the distance–close-up. . . very close–out of the car I was driving!"

"Was somebody hurt?"

"A couple walking on the sidewalk. . . both killed outright."

She thought she saw the beginning of tears in his eyes. "I'm sorry. . . Was it. . . you who shot?"

"No, it was George 'Shotgun' McGurn, but their blood is on my hands just the same."

"Can you tell me about it, Harland?"

"Not here, but let's go out to the place we were in the woods. Then I'll tell you the story."

They continued with their soup and crackers. Harland asked Eleanor, "Methodist? Is that the church you went to in Iowa?"

"No, back home, when we moved to town it was a German church. Some called it Lutheran, but it was really Evangelical–Zion Evangelical."

"So, you're German?"

"My great-grandparents came from Germany."

"Like I said, my family is in Italy and they are Catholic . . . but I'm not anymore."

They finished their soup and left the café. As they entered the familiar trail away from town, deep in thought Eleanor gently took Harland's hand as they walked along.

They sat close on the log. Harland began telling his story immediately. "A man and his wife were just coming out of a restaurant on Milwaukee Avenue. My job was to drive the big black sedan past them allowing the men in the back seat to aim their sawed off shot guns and pull the triggers. Two horrifying shots. The two people were cut down–dead-- splattered on the side walk and I had to drive away as fast as I could so that in minutes we were hidden in the traffic. Oh, Mary, Mother of God. . . what have I done?"

Eleanor had no words, but she took Harland's hand in hers and placed them in her lap. They sat for a time without saying anything to each other. But something must have passed between them which had the effect of drawing them closer and of alleviating Harland's inner pain.

Harland was the first to speak. "I have had no one else who I could have told that to. Eleanor, you are the only friend I have found since coming to America . . . and we have only just met."

"Oh, Harland. I'm glad you feel that way."

"I've dumped a lot of stuff on you. I could never have told all that to a priest in confession. You have been my priest, Eleanor!"

"I don't know what to say."

"You don't have to say anything." He thought of her weeping in the cemetery. "Except maybe to tell me more about yourself. . . like where you hurt."

"Hurt?"

"Or what makes you sad. . . sad enough to weep?"

After thinking about Harland's question she finally told him about a letter she had recently received from somebody she worked with in Chicago. "I got this letter from one of the girls who worked in the soda fountain. Caroline is her name. She told me that one of the girls who worked upstairs had been shot and killed."

"How?"

"By a client." She began to weep. "She was the one my boss made me watch. She was so young. She had gotten on the wrong path, and now she's dead."

"I'm sorry." He hesitated and then asked, "Is that what made you weep at the cemetery?"

"Yes. How'd you know?"

He told her about having seen her at Wilda's grave outside the fence.

"I'd heard about her. Also a very young woman. A prostitute killed by a man she'd been with. They wouldn't bury her inside the cemetery because of what she'd been. So they buried her outside the fence. Poor thing," Eleanor wept. Harland held her hand now in his lap.

"Nothing like that ever happened in the town I grew up in back in Iowa."

"Certainly not in my home village in Italy, either." He thought some more about this. "I should never have come to America."

"And I wish I was back in Iowa. . . but I'd be ashamed to go back."

"And I don't think I could return to Italy. Chicago changed me so much that I am a different person in some ways." He was quiet for a little while and then added, "And, Eleanor, talking with you has helped me to change in another way since I have been here in Illinois City."

"I wonder how that can be?"

"I guess you have helped me get my mind off of what happened back there when I was a hostage in Scarface Al's mob."

"In some ways, I was also under the thumb of the same mob."

"Yeah, they're all over the city, and then some."

At this point the two friends realized it was time to get back to their respective places. After another Sunday together. As they got up,

Harland thought to say one more thing, though hesitantly. "Eleanor, you and I both said we wished we had never gone away from home. . . but now that I think of it, if I had stayed in Italy, I would never have found you."

"Oh, Harland. That's sweet. . . and I can say the same thing."

That night Harland slept more peacefully than he had in weeks. He would later realize that sharing his story with Eleanor had been much like going to confession and receiving absolution from a priest.

Through the coming months, going to church each Sunday morning became a high point in both Eleanor's and Harland's week. As the winter closed in on them, they often had to settle for the hour or so in church, and the walk to and from the church. The snow kept them from doing much walking together in the woods. But a little like the old saying "absence makes the heart grow fonder," the two found themselves more and more drawn to each other.

On a Sunday in early December, they found the Asbury sanctuary decorated for Christmas. A large spruce tree stood to the left of the pulpit bedecked with silver ornaments and golden braided garlands. On the other side was a large evergreen wreath with a big red bow at its bottom. At each window a candle was burning. On the communion table in front of the gold cross a nativity scene had been set up. "Oh isn't it beautiful!" Eleanor exclaimed as she squeezed Harland's hand. "It makes me feel as if I'm in my home church again."

The final hymn was "O Little Town of Bethlehem." As the two friends left the church Eleanor kept humming the familiar and nostalgic tune. "Oh, Harland, I feel so homesick. Christmas was so special at home."

"Tell me about it, Eleanor. All I remember from my home in Italy was my family going to midnight mass."

"Our church always had a Christmas tree like they do here. A few nights before Christmas there would be a big children's Christmas party. Lots of singing of carols, a pageant displaying the story of Bethlehem. And at the end of the program, Santa Claus would come with a big bag, shouting *Ho—ho-ho*. Then he would have a present for each child. . . . ."

"What kind of presents?"

"Usually a little piece of candy or a cookie. One year little dolls made by one of the ladies in the church"

"I thought that an America Santa came to each child's house on Christmas Eve, so wasn't it kind of strange to have him come to church sometime before that?"

"We never thought about that. . . . In Italy, did you have Santa when you were little?"

"No, but we had La Befana. She was an old lady who came the night before Epiphany and brought gifts to the children."

"What's Epiphany?"

"That's when the Wise Men came to bring gifs to the Christ Child on our January 6th." The words of a poem came to Harland's mind. "Viene, viene la Befana."

"My oh my, what does that mean?"

"Here comes, here comes the Befana"

"Do you know the rest of the poem?"

"I used to, but I think I have it on an old Christmas card I got when I first came to the U.S."

"Maybe you could find that. I'd like to hear the rest of it."

They reached the Mayor's house and it was time to part. "Eleanor, I'll look for the poem. You have me wondering now about the rest of it. And I want to know about your Christmas memories from Iowa."

"Next time we get together."

The two parted, both in a bittersweet mood. It was so good to talk together and so hard to have to go their separate ways.

As Harland returned to his carriage house room, he wondered what kind of a lonely experience Christmas would be for him and if there would be any chance of spending some of the time with Eleanor. The fact of the matter was that there were a number of people in Illinois City without any families nearby. This was frequently the case in the early mining towns in Montana.

One day close to Christmas, Father Patrick made a point to speak with his cook and housekeeper, Adeline Parker, the Methodist pastor's wife. "Mrs. Parker, I am concerned about the single folks in town who may not have much of a Christmas dinner. And I think I have an idea of what might be done for them."

"What's that, Father?"

"What would you think if the two churches held a Christmas dinner together for anyone who wanted to come, particularly those who would be alone?"

"Why, I think that would be a wonderful idea. It could be sort of a carry-in dinner, but perhaps I could arrange for the roasting of enough turkeys for the group. In fact I think it would work out best in the basement of the Methodist church. I'll be glad to talk to my husband and we can start planning this, I should think."

"Good. Let's do it."

Christmas came to Illinois City and the dinner sponsored by the two churches was a huge success. It attracted not only singles but whole families as well. Many from each congregation as well as a sizeable group who had not affiliated with either congregation came for dinner. The turkey dinner was complete with all the trimmings and the carol singing which followed was heart warming. There were games for the children and lots of good old visiting for the adults.

Harland and Eleanor spent every bit of the time with each other. The warm holiday spirit of the day drew them together even more closely than ever. "Ever since you got me talking about Christmas back in Iowa I have been wanting to tell you about our Christmas Eve tradition."

"Please do, Ellie."

"Toward evening on the day before, when it was already fairly dark, my father would hitch up our horse to a sleigh and our whole family would bundle up to keep warm on a trip of about an hour to my grandparents farm, which was near where our farm from my early days had been. We would bring the gifts we intended to give to them. I can still hear the bells on the horse as they jingled. The lane we took followed along a stream which was frozen over with lots of snow on its banks as well as on our road. It was especially beautiful on those nights when the moon was out and we could see stars sparkling. But we kids couldn't hardly wait to get there. And when we did, it was so wonderful. Delicious smells from Grandma's kitchen. Candles lit everywhere, a roaring fire in the fireplace. And her fluffy cat, Tobias, asleep in front of it.

"We would then sit down at her dining room table and she would bring out her traditional Christmas Eve supper. . ."

"What was that?"

"Stewed oysters! I don't think I'd want them any other time, but on this night it was special. Then for dessert Grandma brought a big plate of all her different Christmas cookies and fruit cake. Many of the cookies were her German recipes from way back in her family. Lebkuchen Springerles, pfeffernissen. . . I can't remember the other names."

"I wish I'd been there with you."

"So do I." She thought some more about her memories. "Then we would have to go to bed, but early the next morning we'd be up while Grandma made breakfast and Grandpa re-kindled the fire in the fireplace. The stockings hanging from the mantle now looked stuffed."

Eleanor's reverie was interrupted by the announcement that the Christmas dinner would be served. With that Harland and Eleanor joined the rest of the group for a sumptuous dinner.

The sun had set before Harland brought Eleanor to her door. As if by common consent they kissed each other deeply before saying "Good Night" and "Merry Christmas" almost in unison. From that night following they found themselves falling in love as never before in either of their lives.

Those who had planned this community Christmas Dinner were immensely pleased with the outcome of the day and determined to make this an annual event. A resolve which sadly would never be carried out, for unknown to anyone, there were national storm clouds forming in the East, the impact of which would spell the end of Illinois City.

On the Sunday after Christmas, Harland pulled out an old Christmas card from his pocket to show to Eleanor on their way home from church. "I promised to find the full Befana poem. And this is about the time of Epiphany. Wanna hear it?"

"Oh, yes."

Harland read from the card he'd found in his personal stuff from Italy.

> "Viene, viene la Befana
> Vien dai monti a notte fonda
> Come è stanca! la circonda
> Neve e gelo e tramontana!
> Viene, viene la Befana"

The English translation is:

> "Here comes, here comes the Befana
> She comes from the mountains in the deep of the night
> Look how tired she is! All wrapped up
> In snow and frost and the north wind!
> Here comes, here comes the Befana!"

"I like that. Let's you and me celebrate La Befana as well as Santa after this!"

During January in 1929, with Mr. Moretti's permission Harland began expanding his trucking services to include private contracts he was getting up from others in town to supplement what he was carrying for the Mercantile and Café. In an unanticipated way, Harland's cartage business would benefit from the ultimate demise of the town. It was Harland's undisclosed intention to build up enough savings to make it possible for him to marry Eleanor. But much of his business consisted of helping townspeople to move away as the mines began to shut down and workers were laid off.

In early February on a trip into Missoula, Harland purchased an engagement ring from one of the jewelry stores, and on this same trip he found an especially ornate valentine card for his love.

Valentine's Day that year came on a Thursday. Harland persuaded Eleanor to ask for the evening off so that the two could go to the local café for dinner After dinner, when most of the dinner crowd had left the café, Harland and Eleanor had a little time to themselves. Harland turned to Eleanor with a very serious expression. "I want you to know that you have been my savior."

"Harland! That can't be, only Jesus is a savior."

"I don't mean it that way. What I mean is that when you very lovingly listened to my confession about the night I was involved in a drive-by shooting, you took a load of guilt off my heart. I have felt freed of that involvement ever since. I sleep now."

"I know you told me I was like a priest hearing confession. Not being Catholic I guess I didn't fully understand, but the way you say it now moves me down deep inside, Harland. I guess in a small way that was like when I told you about the girls in the rooms above the café. That helped me to get over that musky, horrid feeling."

"I'm glad I could do that for you." He paused and then reached into his pocket. She saw that and went into her purse. He then said. "I have this for you."

"She also said," I have a valentine for you too."

They exchanged valentines. When Eleanor read the message on the card he gave her, she burst into tears after she read the words: *Be my*

Valentine, Be my Love. In the blank space beneath the printed wording, Harland had added: *AND WILL YOU BE MY WIFE?*

She dabbed her hanky at her eyes and smiled. "Yes, Harland–I will be your wife!"

With that he brought out the jewelry box and gave her the ring.

"Oh, Harland. . . ."

"I love you, Ellie, now and always!"

"And I love you Harland, so very much. And I want to be your wife."

Harland took the ring and put it on Ellie's finger. Fortunately it was the right size.

"Harland, it's beautiful."

Harland smiled with pride but then his mood changed. Harland looked troubled. "But, I don't know how soon that will be. I need more in the bank, but with so many leaving town, I am getting more work."

"I'll wait for you as long as it takes."

That would be a promise Ellie would have to hold true to for some time to come.

"Ellie, I don't want you to have to work after we are married. I want to build up my business so that it can support us both . . . and a family!"

"Oh, Harland, that's what I want too. Where do you hope we will live?"

"It won't be here, I know. . . maybe Missoula. . . or Anaconda. What do you wish?"

"I don't know. Just as long as we are together."

At this point the café was near closing time, so the engaged couple got up to leave. When it appeared they were alone they kissed before going to their respective apartments.

CHAPTER 9

Chicago - February 14, 1929

At ten o'clock on a frosty morning near 22nd Street and Michigan Avenue, the location of the Lexington Hotel, headquarters of the Capone syndicate, two large luxury sedans pulled out of a nearby garage and headed north. One was a 1926 Peerless, the other a black 1927 Cadillac sedan, each resembling police cars of the day. A half hour later the two cars pulled up at the SMC Cartage Company at 2122 North Clark Street, one in front and one around back at the garage entrance. Four men, Fred "Killer" Burke, John Scalise, Albert Anselmi, and Joseph Lolordo, jumped out. (Some reports say there were five gunmen.)Two of the gunmen were dressed in police uniforms. With Tommy guns and sawed off shot guns they swarmed into the garage where members of the north side gang of hoodlums under George "Bugs" Moran were working at a secret beer distribution site. Thinking this to be a somewhat routine police raid, the seven men held up their hands and faced the wall as ordered by the surprise intruders. Immediately, following the order as planned by Jack "Machine Gun" McGurn, one of "Scarface" Al Capone's henchmen, multiple volleys were fired into the unsuspecting victims of this gang warfare raid on the morning of St. Valentine's Day in 1929. The two luxury sedans, one of which was a stolen police car, sped away before Chicago police officers could arrive at the scene. When the police officers arrived they found six men were sprawled dead in pools of blood on the cold concrete floor. One of Moran's men tried to escape. However, he had been mortally wounded and died in a nearby hospital an hour later.

While the Capone Mob was universally thought to be the perpetrators of this massacre, no convicting evidence could be obtained, and so no charges were ever made. Neither Capone himself nor Bugs Moran were present at the time of the incident. Capone was at his Florida mansion on Palm Island at the time. His rival, Bugs Moran, lived to see his outfit disintegrate after this violent decimation of his mob. Three years later Moran was sent to prison on other charges.

As a result of this St. Valentines Day carnage, the Capone gang would dominate the entire city of Chicago and surrounding suburbs with its monopoly over illegal alcoholic beverage production and distribution, as well as its extortion based control of many other business enterprises, both legal and illegal, including widespread prostitution and dog-racing.

Montana - 1929

On Friday after Valentine's Day, Harland hauled a truck load to Butte. After unloading, he checked into the Legate Hotel for the night. Before turning in, he went down the street to a little café for supper. Sitting at the counter he picked up a newspaper lying there while he waited for his meal. A cold sweat came over him when he read one of the headlines: *GANGLAND ASSASSINATION OF RIVALS BELIEVED TO BE BY CAPONE MOB.* With his hands shaking he read the news story. This account must surely have brought back to Landi his own implication in a similar situation. So much so that he barely ate his meal.

He turned into his hotel for the night. That night he tossed and turned and had very little sleep. In his sleep he saw McGurn's face and he heard the shots again. He needed his Eleanor.

His mind could not let go of this news of what would be known and remembered forever after as the St. Valentine's Day Massacre. The next morning, as he drove back to Illinois City, his constant feelings were not only of horror and guilt, but fear. Irrational as it might seem he was terrified that some day the mob would find him and do with him what they did to the Moran gang members. *I need to talk to Ellie.*

After his return from Butte, Harland met Eleanor at a mercantile café for supper together. When she saw him she exclaimed, "Harland, you look like you have seen a ghost!"

"I have, in a way. I read in a Butte paper that there was a massacre by the Mob in Chicago killing seven members of a rival gang."

"Oh, my!"

"It brought the memory of my drive-by shooting back into my mind and I can't quit thinking about it. I could hardly sleep."

"I'm so sorry, Harland."

"The awful thing about this is that it makes me worry over my own safety."

"How do you mean?"

"What if they come after me, Ellie. . . ."

"Oh, Harland, they wouldn't do that. . . it's not like you are a threat to them."

"I guess you're right. . . but still. . . ."

Eleanor reached across the table and covered Harland's hand with hers. "You'll be OK."

"Hope so. . . Thanks, Ellie." He felt much better, but there still lurked a shred of fear in the back of his mind.

In the days to come, Harland and Eleanor found as much time as they could to be together. Once again Eleanor's companionship helped relieve Harland of his lingering feelings of guilt as well as fear. He was again sleeping better. However the recent news from Chicago left a residual fear of discovery which he tried to ignore, but found it surfacing in his consciousness frequently.

In an isolated small town such as Illinois City, residents pretty well could recognize whatever vehicles were seen on its streets. A strange car was always a cause for curiosity, especially so when it had "foreign" license plates., which would be any plates from another state, or even another county.

One morning, some weeks later, Harland was alarmed when he saw a black new model sedan pass by slowly toward Main Street, as he prepared to get in the company truck to begin the day's work. He observed a license plate other than Montana, but he couldn't make out what state.

It had been drilled into him when he was driving for Big Al to read the license plates of cars following him or even in the area. "Youse can learn a lot that way, kid." he'd been warned by more than one of Big Al's underlings. "Could keep you above ground!" Surprisingly just as he took his seat in his truck, he remembered another "teaching" from the Mob. "When they come after you, give 'em all youse got, before they make mush out of ya first. Never forget that, kid."

Harland made his way up Main Street until he spotted the strange sedan in front of the café. He noted the Illinois license plate and memorized the number. He parked the truck and went into the café where he saw the driver of the sedan dressed in a black suit sitting at the counter. Harland's first impulse was to leave as unseen as he could. Then the hoodlums' words rang in his ear. *Give 'em all youse got.* With that advice in mind he took the empty stool next to the stranger.

Both men remained quiet while Harland ordered a cup of coffee. He was the first to speak. "My name's Harland. What brings you to Illinois City?"

"My boss wants me to see if we might want to invest in the mines here."

Harland thought this sounded a bit fake. "Not much here any more, sad to say."

"That's what I'm finding out. . . and, oh yes, there's a fella I'm looking for. Heard that he might be living here."

"Oh?"

"Yeah, I've come to inform him of an inheritance which is coming to him. But the attorneys need to locate him."

Harland's first reaction was one of fear. But he dared to ask. "What's his name? Maybe I can help you." Harland steeled himself to remain calm.

"Landino Ferrini. He came to Chicago a few years ago from Italy. Sure wish we could give him what's coming to him."

It was all Harland could do to keep from looking scared and guilty. He pretended to think through all the people he knew in town and then ventured to speak in a casual voice. No one with that name that I can think of."

"Well, I'll ask around and see if anyone else knows him."

At this point Harland could see that he needed to take a more drastic step. He created the impression of still trying to wrack his brain for a Landino. It was then that he remembered that when he had first come to Illinois City people were talking about a mine disaster which had occurred a few months before his arrival. There had been a cave-in which had crushed three miners. He then turned to the stranger and offered . . . .

The stranger could see that he was trying to think. "He might have called himself 'Landi.'"

This gave Harland an opening. He feigned surprised recollection. "Oh, Landi. Now that you mention it there was a Landi who worked in the mines. . . but he was killed in a mine accident. Some timbers collapsed and it caved in on him. They could never retrieve the body. Sorry."

Fortunately this seemed to satisfy the man. In fact he acted relieved. "Well, that settles that. I had begun to doubt whether I'd ever find the guy."

"How long do you expect to stay in town?" Harland asked somewhat furtively.

"I think I'm done here. I'll tell the boss there's nothing here."

"What about that inheritance for Landino?"

"Inheritance?" he seemed mystified at first. "Oh yeah—inheritance. I'll make out a report to the lawyers."

By this time Harland was so relieved that he could quip. "Certainly wish I could have been Landi so that I could cash in."

"Yeah. . . that's an idea. . . Maybe I could pretend and get it myself to take to the kid. Well, been nice talkin' to ya. I'll be out'a here soon as I can gas up the car."

"Right, man. Have a nice trip."

After the stranger left the café, Harland took his time as casually as he could before leaving to go home. Once he was alone and away from others he nearly went to pieces with shaking and overcome with fright. That evening when he and Eleanor had a chance to be together he told her of this terrifying incident. "The thing that I can't get over. Ellie, is that he was actually looking for me! Can you believe it?"

"No. That was close, but it gave you the chance to put them way off the trail for good."

"Yeah."

It was her loving sympathy and her assurance of his safety which finally settled Harland down and enabled him to put this in perspective.

"Harland, sweetheart, your quick thinking saved you from trouble, and I just know that this will be the end of it."

"I hope you're right, Ellie, darling."

CHAPTER 10

Mayor's Mansion - October 1929

Though bed-ridden, Hubert Hudson possessed a clear mind and the ability, though haltingly, to communicate. It was Clara's custom each morning to sit at her husband's bedside to read the Missoulian to him. On Wednesday morning, October 30, 1929 she read the lead article in the Missoulain, regarding the desperate news of what came to be called *Black Tuesday (October 29, 1929)* signaling the stock market crash. When this catastrophic news reached the failing ears of Hubert Hudson, he summoned Laci to join Clara at his bedside. When they were seated at his bedside he began in a voice which was slow and soft due to his physical deterioration. "The news today forces me to take the action I have been contemplating for some time. . .that is to close the mine and mill–permanently."

"Oh, Father, you can't be serious?"

"I am entirely serious, Laci. . . . Our mines are just about played out. Now with the huge losses we are no doubt facing with the stock market crash, we are finished. It makes little difference to me. . . my life is at its end. . . beyond it, I sometimes think."

Now it was Clara's turn to protest. "No. Hubert, you mustn't say that. Don't give up," she said with tears forming in her eyes.

"No, Clara. My mind is made up. There is no other way."

Both knew there was nothing more to be said to try to dissuade him.

In what would be his final directive, he instructed his wife and daughter to cease all operations of the mine and mill and to sell the business including the stock pile of gold and silver still on hand as quickly as possible. "To do this you will need to go to Missoula to consult with our attorney and go to our bank immediately before it is forced to close.

"But, Hubert, you need us here."

"GO NOW. Eleanor will care for me. . . And have our foremen come up here as soon as possible so that I can instruct him to dismiss the men."

A day later Clara and Laci were on board the train leaving for Missoula. News had spread like wild fire throughout Illinois City. A slow-up of the mining operation over the preceding few years had already depleted the population of the town to some extent.

Later that day, as Eleanor sat near Mr. Hudson's bedside, she was summoned to the front door where she opened it to let the mine and mill foremen in. "Hello, Mr. Driscal. Mr. Hudson wants to see you."

"Hello, Eleanor. Is it bad news about his health?"

"Yes, and more." She led them up the stairs to Mr. Hudson's room.

"Mr. Hudson, Your mine foreman is here. You summoned him."

"Yes, Thank you, Eleanor. You may go. I'll let you know if I need you."

Eleanor made her exit as she told Jim Driscal to enter.

"Hello, Jim."

"Hello, Mr. Hudson. You asked to see me."

"Yes, you have seen the national news of the stock market crash?"

"Yes, sir. . . ."

"Well that, along with the failing mines, as well as my own health has led me to make the decision to cease operation immediately. . . .Mrs. Hudson is in Missoula to advise our attorney to prepare to sell the property. He will also see to it that each of our men receive the pay coming to him. . . that is, if you will prepare for Mrs. Hudson the time cards for everyone, yourself included."

"Yes, sir."

"So I want you to inform the men now that we are closing and that they will need to leave Illinois City. . . After all, there'll be nothing left here for them to do."

"It'll be the end of the town."

"That's right, Jim.. . Thank you for all you have done. . . and now, I am tired and need to rest."

"Good bye, sir." With that, Jim Driscal descended the stairs. Eleanor was waiting for him at the foot of the stairs. Her questioning look prompted Driscal to declare. "It's all over. He has ordered me to close everything down."

"Oh my!" was all she could think to say.

He then left by way of the front door.

As a result of this fateful interview the workers at the mine and mill were given notice of the shut-down of operations effective in two weeks. As a result, the remaining families would prepare to leave.

Eleanor would have full responsibility for Mr. Hudson until Clara and Laci would return from Missoula the next day. Knowing his physical condition that responsibility weighed heavily upon Eleanor. After he retired for the night, she felt she should remain close in case he needed her. Sometime after midnight she was awakened by noises from his room. She found him unconscious but very agitated as he restlessly moved around on his bed. She could see that he needed the doctor. The only way she knew to reach the town's physician was to go next door and up the stairs of the carriage house to ask Harland for help. She roused him from his sleep. "Harland, I need your help. Mr. Hudson needs a doctor as soon as possible. I think he may be dying. Could you get him for me?" She was filled with fear and anxiety, which was evident in her voice.

"I'll get him as soon as I can." With that he got up, dressed, and made his way down to Main Street where the doctor's house was located next to the drug store. Harland returned to Eleanor to watch with her until the doctor arrived

She ushered the doctor up to the Mayor's room and returned downstairs to wait with Harland. They sat in silence until they heard the bedroom door close and the sound of the doctor descending the stairway to the living room. "I'm sorry," he said quietly. "He's gone. Nothing I could do. It's trail's end for the mayor." He then asked. "When will Clara and Laci be back?"

Eleanor burst into tears. Harland reached over to comfort her. It was Harland who answered. "On the train tomorrow."

"Good. I'll take care of all the arrangements. But I think I will keep him here until they have seen him once more. You needn't stay around. I'll notify the preacher so that he can meet them at the train and come to the house as soon as they return."

When Clara and Laci stepped off the train from Missoula they were surprised when their Methodist pastor, Rev. Parker, met them on the platform. He led them into the passenger waiting room and to a secluded area where he bid them to be seated. He addressed the mother and daughter, "I am so sorry to have to tell you that Hubert passed away during the night."

"Wasn't Eleanor there to help him?" Clara asked.

"Yes, she discovered him in a agitated state and immediately sent her friend Harland to get the doctor as quickly as he could. The doctor reached Hubert in time to find him still struggling. But could not save him. I am sorry."

Both women were weeping when Clara looked up and said, "First the stroke and now the crash. Just too much for him to take."

"Let me take you both home. The undertaker has left him home for you to say your good-byes."

After the short ride in the preacher's Model "T" up the hill, he led them into the bedroom where he had a prayer with Clara, and Laci and Eleanor as well.

A few days later most of the remaining citizens of Illinois City were gathered in Asbury church for the funeral of their mayor. For many it seemed not only the funeral of their boss but in a sense of their livelihood as well. For, heavy on the minds of all assembled that day was the overwhelming awareness that the closing of the mine and mill constituted trail's end for their town. Whatever in life remained for them would have to be elsewhere. This was verified in the preacher's closing remarks. "Today is trail's end for our city. May God lead us as we find other trails on the journeys each of us must take now as we go from this place. We must pray for the faith of Abraham who went out not knowing to what destination God was calling him."

Afer the close of the service most of the congregation walked in a procession to the cemetery, led by the preacher who was followed by eight men carrying the casket.

Harland stood next to Eleanor and held her hand as the preacher finally intoned, "Dust to dust, ashes to ashes. . . ."

With that the mayor of Illinois City was laid to rest and the people of his town returned to the task of preparing to move on to other trails.

CHAPTER 11

In the weeks following the Mayor's death, Illinois City was fast becoming a ghost town. Pietro was able to arrange passage to Italy for Loreto on a ship which left from Philadelphia. Clara Hudson oversaw the removal of the remaining ore and most of the machinery before officially closing the mine and mill. She and Laci then moved most of their furnishings by freight to Missouri where they would soon join Clara's brother and family. This left Eleanor without income or a place to live until Pietro asked her to come and help out in Etti's place and gave her a room for a few days in the upper floor of the house as long as Morettis were still there.

The Café remained open until the very end and so Harland had some work there for Pietro, who gave him the use of his truck so that he could supplement his income by hiring out to move people and their furnishings. In this way he was able to help the druggist, the doctor and other shop owners to close out their businesses.

The Morettis were the last to move after the final closing of the mercantile and café. Harland and Eleanor helped them load everything of value from both their house and business onto a freight car. Pietro intended to re-establish himself in business in Butte.

On the day of his departure, he summoned Harland to his already empty office in the house. "Harland, you have been a great help to me since you came to Illinois City."

"Thank you, sir."

"What do you plan to do?"

"I thought I might try and find a truck. I hope to get jobs hauling stuff for people wherever I can. I guess I'll start out over in the Bearmouth area and possibly go to Missoula."

"That'll be tough in these hard times, Harland."

"I know, sir, but it's all I know to do."

"What will Eleanor do?"

"She knows of a small hotel in downtown Missoula where she is going to try and get a maid's job. Then she hopes to get enough saved so that eventually she could go back to Iowa where she grew up and where her home is." Harland realized that they had not told the Morettis about their intention to marry. "I guess we haven't told you that we plan to marry as soon as I can save up enough for us to get started out."

"No, you hadn't told us, but Mrs. Moretti and I rather thought you might. Does that mean that you will move to Iowa?"

"We'd like to, but it all depends upon what kind of employment in her home town either or both of us can find."

"We hope it works out for both of you." he said. And then he announced. "I'm going to try to give you a bit of a start. I want you to have my truck."

"Oh, Mr. Moretti, that would be wonderful. How can I ever thank you?"

"Well, I guess now it is a wedding gift from us. You can thank me by making a go of it. And by staying in touch."

"How can we do that?"

"By writing each other. I'll write letters to you at General Delivery in Bearmouth until we get regular addresses. Now I need to say good bye." The older man was obviously afraid of getting emotional. And so with that he gave the keys to the truck to Harland and made ready to leave for Butte. Except for Harland and Eleanor, the Morettis were the last to vacate Illinois City.

The two young people stood on the empty porch of Moretti's house and watched Pietro drive off in his dark green Buick sedan. When the car was out of sight they sat down next to each other on the top step of the empty house. There was a depressing silence between them.

Harland, still holding the keys in his hand, looked at them. "At least we have a way to move out of here."

"I'll be glad to be gone from this place."

"So will I, but I'm even more glad to be gone from Chicago."

"Me too. How about Italy, Harland?. Do you wish you could go back there?"

"Yes, some day. . . ."

"I'd like to go back to Iowa some day. . . but I have to get my life together first. Then maybe after we are married we could go for a visit."

"What's it about Iowa that makes you want to go back?"

She was quiet for a while. "I was happy back there in my family, on the farm and in town, and at school. Ft. Madison, was on the Mississippi River. I loved it when we went down to the river and had a picnic or something. You could see the barges go by and sometimes a river boat with passengers, the kind with a big paddle wheel on the back and two tall smoke stacks. And when its whistle sounded it was thrilling to hear. Then there were the steam trains which went by along the river. I can still hear their whistles. There were two different railroads in the area: the Santa Fe and the Burlington. My father could tell which train it was by the sound of the whistle. Often when I heard the train coming into Illinois City and it blew its whistle, I'd feel sad, thinking about home and wishing I were back there again . . . I never liked it here, until I met you and we got to know each other. . . and fell in love."

"Yeah, meeting you has helped me get over some of my Chicago stuff."

"And now how will we be able to see each other, do you think? If I work in Missoula and you are in Bearmouth."

"We can try as soon as we know what we'll be doing and where." Then he added. "If you get a job at that hotel, and I can haul stuff for folks in Bearmouth, some of those trips would be to Missoula and then we can get together, Ellie."

"Oh, Landi, I hope so."

He looked at her strangely.

"I've been wanting to call you by your original name. Is that OK?"

"I guess so. It's been long enough. They've probably forgotten about me by now."

"Landi! Erase all your Chicago past. You are here now in Montana and we are going to be married. . . soon, I hope."

"I think I will try to get some hauling jobs out of Missoula. Bearmouth won't last long, I don't suppose." Thoughts of the Mob crossed his mind and Ellie could see it.

"But, Landi, you look troubled again."

"I guess I still am a bit fearful. I know I settled that last guy down, but might there be other goons sniffing around for me?"

She looked troubled. "No, Landi! I hope not." He felt awkward. "Shall we put our stuff in the truck and get going?" "Yes, Ellie."

They stood up and without either thinking about it, they hugged. For the longest time. "Elli, I want us to marry just as soon as we can."

"I do too. When?"

"When we both get decent jobs in the same town and save up enough to rent an apartment."

They loaded the truck with what little they had and departed.

They were silent as the truck rumbled down the hill and out of town, passing the old wooden sign which proclaimed: *Trail's End.*

They were moving on.

PART II

Moving On

CHAPTER 12

Eleanor was fortunate to obtain a chamber maid job at a small hotel, the Acme. It was near the railroad station in Missoula. Landi was not so fortunate. After having taken Ellie to Missoula and helping her get her things into a small boarding house near the hotel, they found a small café in which to eat lunch together before Landi had to go back to Bearmouth. Over lunch they discussed their next steps.

"Now that you are settled in a job and a place to live do you feel alright about my leaving you for a few days to do some hauling from Bearmouth?"

"I guess so, but I hope you can get work here and we can be together."

"I'll get a room at the Bearmouth Inn for at least one night until I get some hauling jobs. I don't think I'll be in Bearmouth very long and then I can look for some hauling here. Meanwhile I'll write you a postcard so you'll know what's going on." They finished lunch and rose. They walked back to the boarding house hand in hand. When they came to the steps leading to the door, Eleanor turned to Landi and reached up to put her arms around his neck. "Oh, Landi, I am going to miss you so. You have made me come alive again. I don't want to lose that good feeling."

He put his arms around her waist. "I know, sweetheart. I don't want to be away from you. I think we are meant to be together."

They embraced and kissed before bidding each other "good bye."

Eleanor settled into her new routine with breakfast and supper in the boarding house and work in the hotel from eight in the morning until five in the evening. She shared a room with another young woman about her age. She was Dorothy Visser from Amsterdam, Montana. Fortunately the two hit it off quite well. Both had grown up in farm areas. After high school Dorohy had come to Missoula.

Dorothy had explained, "I came here to go to the university but I ran out of money, so I'll be staying out of school this year to save up enough to go back. What brings you to Missoula?"

"I had a housekeeping job in Illinois City, but the mines closed and everybody moved out. So I came here. My fiancee will come soon after he finishes some jobs he has over at Bearmouth. . . What were you studying, Dorothy?"

"I wanted to be a teacher, so I was in education."

"That's nice. When I left my home in Iowa, I didn't have any plans. I just wanted to get to the big city with all the excitement. I was sick of home."

"What city did you go to?"

"Chicago." Eleanor answered with disappointment in her voice. "But it wasn't exciting. . . at least in the way I had hoped."

"Oh?"

"So I came out to Montana. I certainly didn't want to return to Iowa."

"Why not?"

"Oh. . . my family didn't want me to leave and I was stubborn and went against their wishes. Besides there's nothing there for me, except to apologize for leaving in the first place."

Dorothy then shared her feelings about home. "Me, I'm just the opposite. I wish I were back home. . . and on the farm again."

"Too bad you left? Huh?"

"Yeah. . . I had a boy friend and we were going to get married and stay on his family farm." She paused and seemed to be almost tearful.

"How come you didn't?"

"Jerry was killed in a farm accident."

"OH! I'm sorry."

"That's when I decided to be a teacher."

This would be the first of many serous conversations the two roommates would have as they became friends."

CHAPTER 13

Only a few old timers were left in the tiny town. He found no one who needed any hauling.

One of the few remaining businesses was a rather imposing two storied inn overlooking the Mullan road, on which Landi had traveled from Illinois City to Missoula and back to Bearmouth. He booked one of the few rooms still used for travelers for the night. The elderly clerk at the desk appeared to be the only person around. He went to the empty dining room to see if he could get anything for supper. The desk clerk showed up to take his order. "Hello again. We only have a bit of supper available." He said apologetically. "Hardly anyone stops these days with Missoula as close as it is and Drummond not too far either . . but a few old timers from around here mostly."

"I'm sure I'll get along. What do you have?"

"We've got some chicken a la king on a piece of toast and coffee."

"That'll be fine."

The clerk brought Landi his plate and coffee. And asked. "Mind if I sit down with you?"

"Fine."

The man put his own coffee on the table opposite his only customer and sat down. "What brings you here?"

"Lookin' for work. Came from Illinois City. . . last one to leave."

"I heard it was down completely. Too bad.. We used to get ore from there and other minin' towns to ship on. And so we had lots of business. And we used to be a stage stop on the Mullan, but not any more. What kind of work do you do?"

"Mainly hauling. I've got a truck and I try and pick up and haul stuff for folks."

"Not much here anymore. I guess you've found out."

"Yeah, I guess I'll go back to Missoula tomorrow."

"Missoula? Thought you said you came from Illinois City?"

"I took my girlfriend to Missoula where she's got a job in a hotel."

"I see. . . Let me see. . .I could use some help getting some furniture to Butte. We've closed out a number of rooms and been sellin' the furniture to The Legate there. . .that's about a hundred miles. I believe the Legate is a small hotel on Front Street."

"I could do that tomorrow."

"Good. We'll load you up first thing in the morning. And while you're there, you might check out some work for yourself. Butte's in good shape with the mines and all. Also Anaconda where the smelter is."

"I'll do that."

"In fact I've got a friend who works at the desk of the Montana Hotel in Anaconda. You'll know you're near Anaconda when you see the huge smoke stack of the ACM reduction works. Why don't you stop there and tell him I suggested you ask him. His name is O'Toole–Jimmy OToole. It's on the corner of Park and Main. I'm sorry there just isn't any work for you here."

"If I see O'Toole, I tell him you sent me. And by the way, what is your name?"

"Just tell him Jerry Hogan sent you."

"Thanks. I'll be ready to load at seven in the morning."

CHAPTER 14

Landi arrived in Butte in late afternoon and drove to the Legate. He checked with the manager and was told to stack the furniture at the back door of the hotel He unloaded the furniture and found a small café to stop for a quick lunch. When he paid his bill he bought a post card with a picture of the mines at Butte. He scribbled off a note to Eleanor, and found a mail box before leaving town.

Landi then headed back to Anaconda, which he had spotted about fifteen or twenty miles before he got into Butte. The stack loomed even larger as he passed and drove along Main Street to Park Street. The Montana Hotel dominated the downtown area, and in fact was the largest hotel Landi had seen since Chicago.

As he approached the ornate brick Montana Hotel, from the corner of Park and Main he saw two matching four storied portions of the hotel joined by a single story unit between them with an entry way, most likely leading to a lobby and other common areas inside. The first floor facade of the entire Park Street frontage as well as the Main Street side was made up of nine matching round arches over the windows and doors. Both side portions had rounded corners topped with inverted cone-shaped turrets.

The obvious grandeur of the place had a forbidding effect upon Landi as he drove by looking for a place to park his truck away from the front entry. Landi parked a block away on Park Street, and got out of the truck. He did his best to make himself look presentable and made his way to the steps leading up to the imposing front door of the hotel. He went in and found the reception desk to the side of the lobby. No one was behind the desk, and so he tapped the bell on the desk. A short stocky man in a vested suit came out of a side room and greeted Landi. "How do you do, sir."

"Hello. Do you have a room available for the night?"

"Just for yourself, or do you have a lady with you?"

"I am alone and should be here only one night."

The clerk looked behind a tall partition and then came out and answered. "Yes, we have a room on the fourth floor which is quite nice. It has a $3 per night rate. If you will sign our guest register." He moved the big book in front of Landi and gave him a pen. Landi signed his name as Harland Ferris and indicated his address as Illinois City. The desk clerk gave him his key and pointed to the stairway. "First door on your right on the second floor, sir."

Landi turned around to take his bag and make his way to the stairs. A chill went up the back of his neck when he thought he recognized the man waiting to check in and standing just behind Landi. Fortunately there was no sign of recognition in the man's face. He wore a nicely cut and pressed black suit, unusual for Montana. He wore a gray fedora, also quite unusual. Before going to the stairway, Landi sorted through some newspapers on a table next to an easy chair in the lobby, so that he could continue to observe the stranger. The man left to go up the stairs. Landi took one of the newspapers to the desk clerk while the register was still open giving him a chance to look at the mans's name.

"Yes?" the clerk asked.

"May I take this up to my room? I'll return it next time I come down."

"Certainly, sir."

By that time Landi had seen that the name of the man was, Michael O'Malley, with the address given as Lexington Hotel, Chicago, Illinois. Landi froze. *That's where I've seen him. He's a member of the Outfit. He's used the Mob headquarters as his address. Am I ever glad I used my new name.* While Landi was afraid to be seen by the man, he nevertheless wanted to know what he was doing in Anaconda. Most of all he wanted to know if by chance the man had been sent to find him. To anyone else such a thought would be quite a coincidence, but Landi's guilt and fear made him assume that the man would be hunting him down.

Later, when Landi went down to dinner he stepped outside the hotel and there he saw what was obviously O'Malley's car parked close to the entrance. It was a large black Buick sedan with a red-orange on black

Illinois license plate. On the radiator at the bottom was a small round plate with black letters against a dark orange background. "Veh. Tax Pass Auto." This confirmed Landi's suspicions. That was a Chicago tag.

He returned inside and entered the dining room. O'Malley was seated facing away from him. Landi managed to be shown to a seat at a table near O'Malley's but with his back to O'Malley's back. In this way Landi could hear what the man was saying to the man at his table, without himself being seen.

It appeared that the other man was a local, for he pronounced his town name with an extra "d." "What brings ya to Andaconda?"

"I'm here on business. That's why I asked you to dinner with me tonight. I just got into. town."

"What sort of business?"

In the slight pause the Chicagoan searched for a way to explain without revealing much. "Well, we have an interest in a number of different enterprises throughout the Chicago area and now we are branching out a bit."

"I see."

"They told me you knew just about everybody in town and that you might be able to put me in touch with some of the bosses over at the ACM."

"I might. . ."

The waiter arrived with their dinners, which put an end to their conversation for a few minutes. Landi was also served. Soon he heard the Chicagoan again.

"And oh, by the way.. . do you happen to know a young man by the name of Landino Ferrini?"

Hearing this struck fear into Landi's heart.

"No, I can't say I have. Somebody that's been here in town quite a while?"

"He might have just arrived. . . probably to get a job at the smelter. . . as a watchman, I'd guess."

"Doesn't ring a bell."

Landi made quick work of his supper wanting to be gone by the time the two men would be getting up. Just as he rose from the table he could see that the men were just about ready to leave when the local man said in parting, "I'll let you know when I have a boss you can talk to and if I remember that Italian you mentioned."

"You do that." He sounded menacing.

Landi left as casually as he could. He noticed that O'Malley went up to the desk and was speaking with the desk clerk. When Landi was out of sight, he raced up to his room as quickly as possible and disappeared into his room.

The next morning at 4:30 when Landi went out to put his suitcase in his truck, he found that its tires had been slashed, totally disabling the truck. While standing beside it wondering what to do next, his question was abruptly answered with a blow to his head.

He regained consciousness an hour or so later, blindfolded with his hands tied behind him. He became aware that he was in the rear seat of the Illinois Buick sedan speeding along highway devoid of other vehicles on the road.

CHAPTER 15

A few days after Landi had left to find work in Bearmouth, Eleanor was thrilled to find a post card from Landi in her mailbox. She rushed up to her room to read it

> *Dear Ellie,*
>
> *I just dropped off a load of furniture in Butte. I'm headed back to Anaconda for the night. I'll see if I can pick up any work here. If not, then tomorrow I should be back in Missoula. No more work in Bearmouth, I can't wait to see you*
>
> *Love,*
> *Landi.*

That evening at supper Eleanor told Dorothy about her card from Landi.

"When do you think he'll be getting here?"

"The way I figure it, he should be here in a day or two."

"That's great. I'd like to meet Landi. That's a different sort of name. Is it a nickname?"

"It's short for Landino. He's Italian. He came over here when he was a teenager to work for his uncle in Chicago. . .I'm not sure he was a blood relative or just a family friend whom they called his uncle. He really didn't ever seem to want to talk much to me about his Chicago days. When I first knew him he called himself Harland. He didn't want his Chicago people to find him, I guess."

"Sounds mysterious."

"Yeah, it is. Scary . One time lately some guy from Chicago was looking for Landino and he told him that Landi had been killed in a mine cavein."

"Oh, my! What was that all about?"

"He didn't tell me a lot about his Chicago experience but he said that he had been connected with the Mob."

"The Mob?"

"Yeah, you know the Capone outfit."

"Wow! Is he still in the Mob?"

"No. He escaped and came all the way out here to Montana and tried to disappear. He changed his name. When he told that guy that Landi had been killed, that kept my Landi safe. . I think. . . When he gets back, I'll be relieved."

"I'll look forward to meeting him, Eleanor."

"When he gets back from his hauling job in a few days, I'll introduce him to you."

Over the next few days, Eleanor continued in her work routine, returning each evening to her room eager to check the mail for another card from Landi, or, better yet, to find that he was back to Missoula. But no word. The days turned into a week and still no word.

Ellie began to get nervous about Landi's whereabouts. The only place she knew to check on him was the Bearmouth Hotel, "The last I knew he was on his way to Butte with a load of furniture for the Legate Hotel." She wrote to the Legate, and a return post card said that the load had been delivered.

A few more weeks passed by when Eleanor happened to see a scrap of newspaper from about the time Landi would have been in Butte. It was an Anaconda police report telling of a truck parked in the rear of the Montana Hotel with its tires slashed. When she contacted the hotel in Anaconda, they said that they were aware of the truck but had no idea who owned it. Its licence plates had been removed. No personal items were found to identify it. It had by this time been hauled away. They did not know where it had been taken.

She then asked. "Did you have a Mr. Ferris in your hotel at that time?"

"Let me check."

Eleanor waited nervously while the desk clerk looked through his files.

"As a matter of fact we did."

"Do you have a record of when he checked out?"

Again she waited. "That's strange. We have no record of his checking out, but the next day after the truck was damaged, the room was occupied by someone else. . . and I see here that his bill was unpaid."

"I see. . . Well, thank you. . . And would you contact me if you find anything else about the truck or about Mr. Ferris?"

"Yes, I can do that if you give me your address."

She gave him her address and than thanked him and hung up.

Eleanor threw herself across her bed sobbing. In utter despair she thought, *That was the Mob. I know they often slash tires. By now, I just know my Landi is dead.*

Dorothy came in to find Eleanor on her bed, obviously dismally upset. "Ellie, what's the matter?" Through her tears she told Dorothy about the scrap of news she had found and what it meant.

"Oh, Ellie, aren't you assuming too much? The tire damage may just have delayed him and he will find another way to return to Missoula."

"I wish you were right, but I don't think so. I know the Mob."

"Wait 'til you hear from them, Ellie. I bet there is a good explanation for all that stuff."

"I don't know, but I'm dubious."

Going on the slim thread of hope Dorothy offered, Eleanor waited for Landi to come back. But the longer she waited the more certain she was about her first conclusion.

Then a couple of weeks later she got a piece of mail from the Montana Hotel in Anaconda. She quickly opened it and found what she concluded was her answer.

Dear Mrs. Helm:

Regarding Mr. Ferris room, I have talked with the maid on

duty after he left. She said that the room was in unusual disarray, seeming to reveal a struggle of some kind. On closer examination the next time the room was vacant I discovered what looked like dried blood stains dimly streaked across the wooden floor toward the door. When I contacted the local police regarding these discoveries, they said they would put

the information on file, but that the event had taken place
too long ago for any active investigation to be conducted.

Regretfully,
E..R. O'Keefe, Manager

Eleanor put the letter back in the envelope and began to sob as she concluded in her anguished mind. *The Mob got him, I just know it*

The next time she had a chance to talk with Dorothy, she began by saying.

"Landi has been killed by the Mob. It is all over for me and any thoughts of marriage—to Landi or anybody else."

Dorothy tried to comfort her with a hug, but she did not know what to say.

"It's all over for me here. And I don't know what to do." She spoke in anguish to her friend.

Dorothy tried to help. "Don't you have anyone else? Parents, family?"

"They're all back home in Iowa."

"Could you go back there, at least for a little while?"

"No, I burned all my bridges. It's almost like I ran away. I've never contacted them since I left that night on the bus for Chicago. They wouldn't have me. . . ." *Or would they?* She thought to herself.

Dorothy picked up on Eleanor's hesitation. "You sure?"

"Well, no, not exactly."

"Think about it, Ellie."

That evening Eleanor thought about her conversation with Dorothy and her advice. Her dream that night was a surprisingly accurate tour of her childhood house—the house on Avenue I.

In Eleanor's dream her memory of the house of her childhood was vivid still.

It was a large two storied house with the second floor the same size and shape as the first floor. It was close to the sidewalk along the street called Avenue "I." It was unpaved with a single railroad track running in the center of the street.

As you entered the house, you stepped up onto a front porch and came to the front door on the left hand side of a porch. The door opened into a small hallway with a stairway on the left leading up to the second floor. On the right was a door leading into a formal parlor. The one thing she remembered about that room was the wind-up Victrola. The one record she remembered was "La Paloma." When you walked past the stairs you came to a door which opened into a family room with lots of comfortable couches and chairs. To the right was a bedroom. Walking through the sitting room you came to a dining room on the right and a kitchen ahead. Off to the right of the kitchen was another stairway leading upstairs. At the foot of these stairs was a small bathroom.

Taking the back stairs on the second floor, there was a little bedroom next to the bathroom. A large bedroom occupied the right (west) side of a long hall. I remember it as very sunny with a huge rag rug. There were four other bedrooms up there. At the very front was a tiny sewing room. The long upstairs hall ended with the front stairs leading down to the front door.

The back door was located in the far corner of the kitchen. Another door went out onto a screened-in porch on the side of the house with a long driveway leading to a large barn-like garage at the back of the lot.

Her dream had been so vivid that when she awakened the next morning she was overcome with the desire to see her house again.

Once again Eleanor had come to a trail's end as she thought about leaving Missoula. This time she was utterly alone. And more profoundly, Eleanor found herself at the end of her rope. Three years earlier she had cut the cords which had bound her to her family and to her childhood, both of which she thought she had left behind when she boarded the bus for a new life in Chicago. Disillusioned with Chicago she had fled to Montana carrying her aspiration for a new life into the decaying mining area west of the Rockies. With the depletion of the mines and the tragic loss of Landino, all hopes were dashed.

Now what? Nothing left for Eleanor but to return to the home of her childhood. She quit her job at the Acme and notified her boarding house of her intention to leave.

On the night of her last day at the Acme, Eleanor returned to her room and began packing the few things she had before checking out the next morning. She found a slender chain which had been on an inexpensive necklace. She removed the little cluster of cheap beads which hung on the necklace. She then removed her engagement ring from her finger, kissed it and strung the tiny chain through it and put it around her neck. It hung low enough so that it could be worn under her clothing and not be seen by others. But she would always know it was there near her heart. As she took this decisive step, she thought, *I remain engaged to Landi. That will not change. I belong to him. We shall meet again in the afterlife and then we shall be married for eternity.*

CHAPTER 16

She had decided not to write first. She feared rejection. The more she had thought about it, the more she felt that any letter from her would not even be answered. Then where would she be? She wouldn't even phone from the bus station. She would walk to the house on Avenue I and simply appear at the door.

And so Eleanor packed up what little she intended to take with her, and she disposed of the rest of her life in Montana. She spent her final evening in Montana visiting with Dorothy. "You helped me make my decision to go home."

"I'm glad. I just think you need to get things ironed out with your family. Who will be there, do you suppose?"

"Mother and Father, and my sister. I don't know what to expect. At the worst they may have disowned me and I'll not be welcome. Then I don't know what I'll do."

"Oh, Eleanor, I hope it's not that way. I bet they'll be glad to see you."

"I hope you're right."

"Well, I better get to bed. I need to get up early to catch the bus."

"Sorry. I'll miss you."

"So will I."

"Will you write me?"

"I will."

With that the two friends hugged.

"Where's your engagement ring, Ellie? You haven't lost it?"

"No." She pulled the chain up from beneath her dress. She showed the ring to Dorothy. "I'm always going to wear this, but where no one will see it, because Landi is gone. But, one day, even in heaven I'll put it back on when we are married–forever." She replied with tears in her eyes.

"Oh, Ellie. That's so sweet--bittersweet. You make me teary-eyed too."

They hugged again and bid each other good bye.

The next morning Eleanor boarded the bus for Iowa.

After a day and a night on the bus, the closer she was getting, the more unsure of herself she felt. The scenery outside her window was looking more familiar now. The same as she remembered it. *But I myself am so different from the day I left. That awful time in Chicago really changed me. And Montana wasn't all that good . . . . until I met Landi. With him I felt as though I had grown up and really blossomed. The future looked bright. . . then that dark curtain was swept across my life and my future when Landi was taken away from me.* She had given him up for dead . *Nowhere to turn. . . except back to Iowa. But what if they don't even let me in?*

The bus slowed down as it came into town and very slowly eased it's way into the terminal. Her destination. Eleanor was overcome with a terrifying panic. She was seriously tempted to remain on the bus and forget about trying to go home.

The driver pulled up to a complete stop, shut off the engine and opened the door opposite his seat. Two or three passengers got up and made their way to the door. Timidly, Eleanor rose to get her cheap fake leather-sided suitcase from the rack above her seat, and began her walk to the front and down the steps onto the side-walk. She followed two of the women passengers into the women's room in the station waiting room. She stood before the mirror for a long time trying to straighten her hair and clothing after the long two days in the coach seat. When she returned to the platform, the last of a small group of passengers were entering the bus. She thought about the day when she had left on the bus for Chicago. She shivered to think about the emotion of that departure and the. disappointments which followed. She watched the door close and heard the engine start, and then the bus left the station on its way to Chicago. By this time all those arriving except Eleanor had been met by family or friends, and were on their way.

Alone, Eleanor began her ten block walk to the house on Avenue "I." It had been her childhood home. *Would it be my home again? Or just a house?*

Not walking very fast on this momentous trek, her pace slowed as she came closer to her destination. It was a bittersweet walk for this home town girl. The old familiar houses along the way brought back pleasant memories, but at the same time she felt a deepening regret over having left as she had a few years ago. These scenes, once hers, now belonged to others—no longer hers.. *Could all this be mine again? If only Landi had lived to return with me. We could have started all over. . . whether mother and father would take me back or not. . . If they're still here!* She thought as the house came into view. Instinctively slowing her pace, she approached the sidewalk leading to the porch of the house she once occupied as a child and a youth.

Steeling herself against rejection, Eleanor Helm walked up onto the porch and stepped forward to the door and rang the doorbell. She heard it ring inside, but that was all she heard. *Maybe they're not home.* She almost wished that were so. By this time she had about talked herself into being rejected by her parents. Then she heard steps coming down from the second floor. Eleanor braced herself as the door opened. A woman in what looked like a nurse's apron appeared. "Yes?"

"Are Mr. & Mrs. Helm in?"

The woman hesitated.

"I'm their daughter."

"Oh! Mrs. Is upstairs. . . in bed. But, didn't you know? Mr. Helm has been gone for about a year now."

"Gone?"

"Uh. . . he passed away."

"Oh my.. . May I see Mrs.?"

"Won't you come in?"

Eleanor came in and was ushered into the parlor on the right of the entryway, where she put down her suitcase. When they were seated the woman introduced herself. "I'm Miss Evans. . . Anne."

"I'm Eleanor. I have been away from home for three years. . . out of touch, really."

"That's what I assumed. The fact of the matter is that your mother is 'out of it.' I am afraid she won't know you, Eleanor. She began to slip mentally soon after your father passed away."

"Oh. . .I'm so sorry. . ." She held back the tear which had begun to form.

"But, I know you want to see your mother. So come follow me up to her room. We'll try and see if there is any recognition."

Eleanor followed Anne up the familiar staircase and down the hall to the master bedroom on the right. It was an emotional shock to see her mother in bed, looking so frail. She appeared, however, to be awake when Eleanor stepped around to the window side of the bed to come up close to her mother. She leaned over. "Mother, I've come home." There was no indication of any recognition, only a liquid glassy stare into nowhere.

Anne stepped up and put her arm around Eleanor and led her to a padded rocking chair near the bed. "You better sit down."

Eleanor put her hands up to her face and began to sob. The door downstairs opened and immediately Anne got up and went down to meet Emily. "You should know that your sister has returned and is upstairs with your mother."

A life-shaking shock bolted through Emily. She did not know what to say.. . or to think. She became incensed and shouted out. "I don't want to see that deserter again. She left me holding the bag."

Anne tried to quiet her, fearing for both Eleanor and her mother. "Hush. She might hear you."

"I don't care." Instead of going upstairs, she went back into the family room and sat down to collect her thoughts. Anne followed her into the room and sat down opposite Emily.

Eleanor's sister began to unravel her thoughts, using Anne as a sounding board. "I worried about her at first. Then I would imagine all sorts of things about where she was and what she was doing. Mostly exciting things I wished I were doing. Then when Daddy died I became angry at her for not being here with us for his funeral. Then when Mom got so bad I resented Eleanor for not being here to help take care of her. Now she's here and I don't know what I think. I don't even know if I want to see her."

"But, Emmy, you must."

Eleanor recognized her sister's voice when she entered the house. And she realized Emily's anger at her. At this point she did not want to see her. She slipped down the back stairway and out the side door. She slipped into the front foyer and grabbed her suitcase. and made her way downtown as fast as she could. She obtained a hotel room downtown at the Anthes Hotel for herself until she could collect her thoughts and decide what she would do next.

After a quick bite of supper in the hotel café, Eleanor closed herself in her room, sprawled out on the bed fully clothed, worn out physically from her travel and wrung out emotionally from what she had found at home. Blocking it all out of her mind, she fell asleep.

CHAPTER 17

Sometime in the night, Eleanor was awakened by a low pitched boat whistle which in her dream seemed to be from a steamship sailing away from a harbor and into an unknown expanse of ocean. Someone had been waving, but she couldn't be sure who. And then all she could see was only the darkness over the ocean.

In the darkness of her hotel room, Eleanor sat up in bed and uttered in anguish, "I will never see Landi again. . . he's dead." She'd heard the whistle again. This time she knew it to be from a river boat passing by on the nearby Mississippi. She remembered the sound from her childhood. *It is an omen. That they have killed my Landi. The Mob.* She sobbed herself to sleep, holding his ring on her necklace.

Later in the night, she awakened to find that she was still dressed. She removed her shoes and slipped off her wrinkled dress and buried under her blanket for the remaining hours of the night.

Finally the night was over. She dressed again and made her way downstairs to the café. She felt strangely out of place as she ate her oatmeal and drank her cup of coffee. When she left the hotel she walked along the fog-enshrouded street leading down to the river front where she found a bench on a pathway in Riverview Park. This did not seem like her home, nor did anywhere else. An edge of panic began to creep into her consciousness. *This is not home as I hoped for. Everyone is a stranger – even my sister, and my mother. I feel a stranger to myself. Like it wasn't me out there in Montana. And the girl who lived here before isn't me either.* Eleanor felt an emptiness she had never before felt. Without knowing it, hers was an emptiness waiting to be filled with a new sense of self.

Eleanor got up from her bench and began walking along some of the old familiar streets, walking by houses in which she remembered her childhood friends had lived. She found herself wondering what had become of various old acquaintances—what they were doing now, where they might be living.

After two or three blocks, she came to her church on 10th Street— St. John's. On impulse she walked up the front steps and found the doors were unlocked. She stepped inside and entered the silence of the sanctuary. The dim light coming through the stained glass windows, together with the pungent aroma of oil mopped floors and from the richly polished ancient pews. This sacred space filled her with vivid memories of having spent many Sunday mornings in this sanctuary as a child and later as a youth Eleanor took a seat in the pew her family had always occupied. She bowed her head and let the memories flood into her emptiness.

She was eight years old again and sitting next to her mother on one side with sister Emily on the other side. Her father was in the choir at the front of the church. She had on her favorite Sunday dress, a frilly blue which she always wore with her white stockings and patent leather buckle shoes. She was listening to the melodic sound of the pipe organ quietly drifting over the congregation gathering for worship, the familiar voice of the preacher announcing Hymn No. 185, "My Jesus, I Love Thee." The organist brought back the familiar melody with her mother singing so clearly in her comforting soprano voice: "My Jesus, I love Thee, I know thou art mine. . . ."

Tears formed in her eyes as she felt transported back to a time of uncomplicated happiness in her little life. Now the music ended and the sun-lit sanctuary became restfully quiet. A slight creak in the floor and then a voice brought her suddenly back into reality. "Oh, I hadn't known you were here. I didn't mean to interrupt your meditation with my playing. So sorry."

Startled, she looked up into the face of a young man about her own age. He wore a white dress shirt with the sleeves rolled up, a maroon tie and gray woolen pleated trousers. His worried smile seemed to reach down to where she was sitting. He looked into her eyes and added, "Are you troubled? May I see if the pastor can see you?"

"Oh, no. I'll be all right. But, thank you." She then added an explanation, "I used to live here.This was my church, and I guess a lot of memories came rushing into my thoughts."

"I know what you mean. Sometimes when I play a certain hymn, it brings back a flood of memories."

"Yes.. . for me too. In fact it was a hymn that triggered memories for me just a bit ago."

"What hymn was it. . .Oh, I shouldn't intrude like that."

"No, it was *My Jesus, I Love Thee"*

"I know it well." He paused, as if in thought." "Well, I must get back to my practice. . . that is, if I won't disturb you."

"Please go ahead. I like to hear you playing. . . in fact, would you mind playing *My Jesus. I Love Thee?"*

"Glad to. . . by the way, I'm Ernest-- Ernest Hauser."

"I'm Eleanor Helm."

A curious recognition came to him which he did not acknowledge."Nice to meet you . . . Let me know if you need anything." With that, the organist returned to the organ and began by playing the hymn Eleanor had requested.

She let herself be bathed in the music and inspired by the words. She sat quietly while Ernest turned to another hymn and began to play *Jesus is Tenderly Calling Thee Home.* Eleanor remembered some of the words, enough to feel the tug on her heart of the phrase, *Calling Me Home.*

I've come home, she thought as she got up to leave the church building.

As she made her way back to her hotel, Eleanor thought about Emily. *When you come down to it, Emily's feelings about me are all my fault. Not hers. I'm the one who deserted her and left her with responsibility for our parents.* With that she resolved to go to Emily as soon as she saw her and try to make amends. But she did not know quite how she would approach Emily.

As she left the sanctuary and walked down the steps of St. John's church, she resolved to return for worship the next Sunday. However, she did not know what to expect when she saw her sister at church. But, she thought *I am just going to have to patch things up with Emily, We can't remain cut off from each other. Maybe I can talk to her after church.*

When Sunday came, Eleanor walked to St. John's and decided to sit in the area of the church where her family had always sat–about half way down on the right side. She was a bit early and so found "their pew" vacant. She eased herself into the center of the pew. *I wonder if Emily still sits here.* This thought made her apprehensive. She soon found Emily making her way down the aisle. She paused at Eleanor's pew, and then entered. Eleanor greeted her sister somewhat formally. "Good morning, Emily."

"Good morning," Emily said without looking and continued to stare at the floor.

Eleanor's instinctive inclination was to try to engage Emily in some small talk, at least, but Emily's demeanor made her drop the idea. *But after the service I really ought to say something.* In the meantime, Eleanor tried to concentrate on the worship. After the benediction as the organist began to play a postlude, Emily gathered up her purse and began to move toward the aisle. Eleanor reached over and touched her arm. Emily looked at Eleanor who pleaded, "Won't you give me a moment or two. I want to say something to you?"

"What?"

"I know I can't make amends to you, but I want you to know how awfully sorry I am, to have dumped everything on you. . . Nothing in my life since leaving has turned out to be any good. I am here to try and start over. . . I know you probably don't accept that, but let me at least offer this to you."

"What's that?"

"I would like to take over the night duties at home with Mother, so that you can be free of that."

"Uh huh. Yeah, you can do that." Under her breath, "It's the least you could do." Then she added. "You gonna visit Mother today?"

"If that's ok."

"Sure, it's OK. . . You might just as well come with me now."

As it turned out, Emily was appreciative of Eleanor's offer to take over the night duties regarding their mother's care which had tied Emily down for some time. It would be some time before the two sisters would become close again, but this new arrangement of sharing their mother's care would go a long way toward reconciliation. As it was Emily was employed on the day shift of Schaeffer Pen, and having her nights free was a gift Eleanor could give her.

CHAPTER 18

Chicago 1931

Following his abduction at the hotel in Anaconda, Landi's trip back to Chicago remained a blur in his memory—a bad memory. He had no idea of when he regained consciousness. Never out of sight of the Mob thugs, he was finally delivered to the Hawthorne Hotel in Cicero where some of the higher-ups took charge of him. They brought him upstairs to Capone's headquarters. His appearance before Big Al reduced him to emotional pulp. On threat of his being rubbed out by the Mob, he was directed to have no contact whatsoever with any of his contacts in Montana. That, of course, included Eleanor. He was to resume his duties as driver for the Mob, and assigned a room in the Hawthorne—a location in which he was under constant surveillance.

After his violent return to Chicago, Landi was forced to settle into the routine of a driver for the Mob once again, but this time not for Big Al himself. During this time he cautiously made repeated attempts to communicate with Eleanor back in Missoula, Montana. He believed that any mail which he received at the hotel would be examined by Big Al's people. Rather than risk such disclosure, he thought that a post office box would be best for him, but how to arrange for a box unseen by the Mob had been a problem. The break came one day when Fred Nitti summoned Landi.

"Hey, kid, I want you to mail this envelope for me at the post office sub-station. You know where that is?"

"Yeah, I do."

"I want you to take this when no one sees you. Now's as good a time as any. Walk, don't take the car. And use the rear door." He handed the envelope to Landi.

"Yes sir."

Landi saw this as his chance. In his room he hurriedly wrote a note to Eleanor, and quickly went down the stairs to the rear door, and began his walk a few blocks to the post office. He mailed the envelope and his note. He then signed up for a P. O. Box.

Fortunately he would be sent on a number of errands on foot, and so had chances to check his box every so often. However, much to his disappointment, his letters were returned to his post office box as undeliverable. This frustrating loss of connection compounded the guilt which had built up in Landi's consciousness over not having been able in any way to correspond with Ellie after he had been abducted by the Mob and brought back to Chicago.

His next attempt would be to try and identify the hotel in which she worked to see if he could reach her at her work. He remembered that it had been the Acme on Front Street near the N.P. Depot. However before he got a letter off to the Acme, he came across a news item in a current newspaper which shook him to the core. He spotted a headline at a news stand.

NO SURVIVORS IN HOTEL FIRE IN MONTANA.

Missoula, Montana. A mid- morning fire swept through
The Acme Hotel this morning, completely destroying the
structure and snuffing out the lives of eighteen
employees and twenty-six guests. The following is thought
to be an accurate listing of the names of the staff and of
guests at the time of the tragic fire.

Panicked, Landi found *Eleanor Helm* on the list. He was overcome with grief entangled with guilt and could barely finish his assigned trips for the day. His driving duties were mind-numbing, and often terrifying as he remembered the drive-by shooting which had so sickened him in the past. However, forces beyond his control or the Mob's control would spell the end of Landi's assignments, much to his relief.

Following a long trial, on October 17, 1931 the jury returned a verdict, finding Alphonse Capone guilty of five counts of tax evasion and failing to file tax returns. The judge sentenced him to 11 years imprisonment. Capone's trial and conviction on October 17, 1931, threw the Mob into turmoil. The ensuing confusion in the Mob provided Landi the opportunity he had been looking for to make his break and disappear.

During the night after the conviction, Landi packed as much of his clothing as he could in a small valise and furtively left his room and quietly climbed down the outside fire escape on the back wall of the Hawthorne. Once on the alley, he made his way stealthily to the nearest "L" station. He boarded the next train which took him to the Loop. Down onto the street he walked to the La Salle Street Station. He hurried to the first ticket window he came to, where he was able to purchase a one way ticket on the Rock Island Line. He asked the agent where he would be most likely to find work.

"I would suggest the town of LaSalle, just a couple of hours away. They have some industry there. There is a train leaving for LaSalle in an hour."

"I'll take it."

Landi kept moving about the terminal hall as he awaited the boarding time, always carefully surveying to see if he spotted anyone from the Mob who might have followed him. He was much relieved when his train was called. He rushed onto the platform. He climbed onto the first available coach. He relaxed only after the train began to move.

In the time it took to reach his destination, Landi worked out a tentative plan. His ultimate goal was to go as far away from Chicago and the Mob as possible. He would find what work he could and save enough for passage back to Italy. He simply did not feel safe anywhere in the U.S. All the while he would keep as low a profile as possible. He did not know whether any of his family were still in the region of his origin, but quite possibly there would be cousins. He thought also of Loreto and Armando. *I think I can locate them since they will most likely have gone back to Loreto's home. In fact they may well be living in the same village as some of my cousins.*

He tried to force thoughts of Eleanor out of his consciousness, now that he felt certain she had been lost in the fire. He couldn't bear to think of fire consuming her. If only he could have gotten back to

Missoula in time for them to move somewhere else—anywhere but the room which must have been her fiery grave. Overlying his stinging emotions of fear of the Mob and grief over his loss of Ellie, he felt a desperation. He yearned for a totally new start. He was convinced that such a new beginning could only be found in his return to Italy, the only other spot on the face of the earth he knew.

After arriving in LaSalle, he stepped out of the train station and headed up the hill to downtown LaSalle. He needed to find a room and a job. He checked into the Kaskaskia Hotel which he spotted on his walk. It would be too expensive for more that a night or two, but it gave a temporary room. He asked the desk clerk, "Can you tell me where I might find a job of any kind?"

"Well, the chief employment here would be the M& H Zinc over on the east edge of town, or Westclox just west in the adjoining town of Peru. . . You say you'll do anything?"

"Yes."

"You might go back in our kitchen and find the chef to see what he might have."

"Thank you, I just might do that as soon as I get my stuff upstairs and clean up a bit."

"Just through that door over there," he pointed toward the dining room.

As a result of this exchange, Landi found a job as a dishwasher in the Kaskaskia. It would be a job in which he would be pretty much alone, which suited him.

The next day he rented a tiny apartment in a house on Zinc Street. He felt safe and settled at least temporarily. His dishwashing job was from mid-afternoon until 10 or 11 after the two main meals of the day. This gave him a chance in good weather to take walks around town, which were a relief from being cooped up in his tiny room. His schedule at the hotel also provided him lunch and supper—not from the menu, but whatever the cooks gave him. Breakfasts usually consisted of a doughnut and coffee at a cafe along his customary walk. In contrast to Chicago life was good—on the surface. But underneath Landi grieved over his loss of Eleanor.

Among the precious memories he had of his time with Ellie were their Sundays together. Going to church with her and so many long talks afterwards. On one particular morning after Landi had had some sorrowful dreams of Ellie, he walked past a church on 4th Street. Trinity Church was the name on its bulletin board. On impulse he walked up the front steps and entered the sanctuary. At first he had thought it was a Catholic Church, but then concluded it to be Protestant of some variety. He found some comfort in the peaceful quiet of the place and sat in a pew for a while thinking about Eleanor. *Will I always have to be alone. Could there ever be someone else. . .I wonder, but I don't think so. Perhaps I'll meet someone in Italy.*

During his time in LaSalle, he often thought of his childhood home in Italy. This made him all the more eager to find a way to return. Living very frugally and working as much overtime as he could allowed him to save. It took him longer than he had hoped to save enough to return home to Italy. But after some months he counted his savings and realized that he could make his return to his home land.

After terminating his work at the Kaskaskia and closing out his room on Zinc Street, Landi packed what little he had in a suitcase and boarded the Rock Island for Chicago and then walked to Union Station and boarded a New York Central for New York City. He found a freighter bound for Italy and booked passage on it.

It was to Angri that Landino fled after arriving in Italy, and ultimately traveling a few miles to the northwest where he disappeared into the anonymity of Naples.

Landi worked at a variety of jobs driving delivery trucks throughout Naples and the surrounding communities on the Bay of Naples. In the course of his deliveries, he came to know the owners of the LaMedusa Grand Hotel about twenty miles southeast of Naples. This acquaintance eventually resulted in Landi taking a job there as a desk clerk, a position he would keep for his remaining years in Italy.

In the quiet of the Italian countryside and along the stunning Mediterranean shore of the Bay of Naples, Landi spent much of his free time walking the hills and the sandy beaches. In his solitary hours he could not hold back the tides of guilt which washed over him repeatedly. In some ways his guilt intensified after he had concluded that Ellie had died in the hotel fire.

Unable to shake off his feelings about what he assumed was Eleanor's death, he went to the local priest about this. The priest advised him to create a little shrine somewhere to honor his fiance's death. Landino returned to his walled garden behind his house and took some rocks and made a small circle in one of the corners. Within the circle he placed a small flat rock on which he had painted the name *ELEANOR*. This devotional act gave Landi some sense of closure. But he would continue to have night dreams in which Eleanor appeared.

CHAPTER 19

The day after the fire in Missoula, while seated at her breakfast table, Elleanor read about the tragedy in the local paper. It was a shock to her to see her name listed as among the staff who were presumably lost in the fire. She gave a word of thanks that she had left Missoula and had not been in the hotel at the time of the fire. She prayed for the families of those who died in the fire. She then went upstairs to sit beside her mother.

Over the next few months, Eleanor settled into a routine. She became better acquainted with Anne Evans, who had been caring for her mother since she had begun to fail both mentally and physically. Eleanor took over meal preparation and took Anne's place after she left each day around four o'clock and returned at eight in the morning. In the course of their cooperation, they became good friends. In time, Emily and Eleanor became sisters to each other again, but still not close.

What Eleanor could not fathom was what her own future was to be. Emily had a steady boyfriend and it looked as though they were headed for marriage. While her mother remained alive she had become Eleanor's reason for being. *But then what?* She was almost ashamed to ask herself. Anne would work for another family with a bedridden loved one. The bank was handling Mrs. Helm's funds and financial needs. As part of the household Eleanor's basic needs were covered. *But what is ahead for me?* She was hesitant to talk with Emily about these questions for fear of sounding as if she was after her part of the inheritance, whatever that was.

Meanwhile Eleanor received a great deal of support from her regular attendance at her church. Her worship attendance and participation in other church activities gave her opportunity to develop relationships with others, some from her former times and others were new friends.

One new acquaintance was Ernest Hauser, the church organist. She had gotten accustomed to seeing Ernest at the organ each Sunday during worship and didn't think much about it. Then one Sunday she met him outside the church as she was preparing to walk home. "Hello, Eleanor. I haven't seen you talk to since that time we met during my practice."

"No, that's right. But how nice that you remembered my name. . . .Ernest, is it?"

"Yes. . . May I give you a ride? My car is just across the street."

"I guess so. Is that your car over there with a leather folding roof?"

"That's it. Ever seen one like that?"

"No, but it's a cute two seater."

When they got in the car Ernest asked, "Where may I take you?"

"On Avenue I a little west of here. I'll tell you when we get there."

"You're new in town?"

"Yes, I just returned from Montana, but I grew up here—in fact, in the house I am in now."

"Montana! Getting rich on the gold there?"

"Not at all, even though I was in a gold mining town for a while, just as a servant girl. The town went bust when the mines played out. Then I moved to a bigger town where I was a chambermaid in a small hotel. That wasn't getting me anywhere, so I came back. Found out that my father had died and Mother has senility. So here I am, sort of at loose ends. . . which explains how you found me that day in a pew while you were playing." she felt embarrassed about having told so much of her story to this stranger. Hastening to change the subject she asked, "How about you? Have you lived here long?"

"All my life, except after high school I moved to a little town nearby to work in an auto garage there, but I soon moved back here to work for the Ford garage as a mechanic."

"Oh, so this is a Ford?"

"No, it's an Auburn 8/100 Roadster—1927."

"Never heard of an Auburn."

"They are rare."

"I thought maybe you were a music teacher on your own or maybe at the school."

"No, playing the organ is a hobby, I guess. I started when I was kid, and at then after I returned here to work at the Ford Garage, I was offered the job to play at my church, St. John's. I took the job. But my real job is working on automobiles, which I really enjoy. Not that I don't enjoy playing the organ. I do."

"You still work at the Ford garage ?"

"No, I have my own shop now. I work out of the garage in my back yard."

By this time they were coming near Eleanor's mother's house. "I'm going over there, to that large white house."

"You live there?"

"No, but my mother does and I'm taking care of her."

"Why, that's where Emily Helm lives!"

"Yes, I'm her sister."

"Really!"

"I'm not surprised. We aren't on the best of terms right now. That's why I don't live there. I live in a downtown hotel for the time being.

"Oh?"

Avenue I is an unpaved dirt street with a single railroad track down the middle. Ernest drove to the end of the block and made a u-turn so that he could stop in front of her house. When he stopped, she opened her door to step down on the grass. "Thank you, Ernest, for the ride home."

"My pleasure. Call me 'Ernie' by the way."

"Bye, Ernie."

"See you next Sunday."

She fixed a light lunch for herself and then took over sitting with her mother for the rest of the afternoon and evening. This gave Eleanor a long uninterrupted time to ponder her life and her present situation, as she sat in a wooden rocking chair by the sunlit window of her mother's bedroom. In the quiet of a Sunday afternoon, the only sound she heard was the steady breathing of her mother as she slept. Asleep or awake, her mother was unresponsive. All one could do was to care for her basic needs and comfort. Otherwise she was gone, leaving Eleanor only memories of what she had once been.

It was very painful to Eleanor to think that despite her returning to her mother and her home, whatever awareness her mother still possessed was of the disappearance of her daughter. She had been unable to renew life with her parents upon her return to Iowa. Both were gone from her life, even though one lay in the bed next to her. This frustration kept Eleanor from being able to think ahead to any future for herself.

Both Chicago and Montana left her with the dull ache of unrealized expectations. In that almost dream-like haze which comes sometimes when one sits quietly in silent surroundings, she let her mind review her life so far. *I thought I would find an exciting life and career in dazzling Chicago. Places to see—new friends—my own apartment in an attractive neighborhood in the city—money enough to buy nice things I wanted. . . . . None of that happened to me. . . . Escaping to Montana would bring new experiences and a new life. . . new but not so good. . . . and then love and marriage to Landi. . . . For all I know, he's dead. . . . the Mob stole that dream from me also. Here I am, home again. . . . I can't even remember what it was I expected when I was a little girl, playing with my dolls on this very sunlit floor. . . . whatever it was didn't come true.*

Her reverie came to a halt and she assumed normal consciousness when she was struck with a thought. *Maybe it's me! Always thought it was my situation that needed changing.*

Just then the front door bell rang, the kind which is mounted on the door and it rings when a handle is twisted. Eleanor stirred herself and went down stairs to open the door.

It was Ernie. "Oh, hello, Ernie?"

"Hello, Eleanor." He seemed embarrassed. "I came by to see how you are. . . you seemed so down when I left you off .. . Like when we first met during my practice. . . Maybe I shouldn't ask. . . I know it's none of my business."

Now Eleanor was embarrassed. "That's alright. . won't you come in?"

"You sure I should?" he said as he stepped across the threshold and closed the door behind him.

"Sit down here in the parlor. I can talk a few minutes, but then I must return upstairs to Mother." He seemed to question her. She explained "She's bedridden and is also mentally gone."

"Does she know you have come back?"

"I'm not sure. It is the way I found her when I returned home. Ernie, that's a big part of what is troubling me deeply now, as well as the fact that my father died before I got to see him again. So-o-o, I'm in a kind of unhappy period of my life after getting home."

"I'm sorry, Eleanor."

"I know and I appreciate your concern. . ." She appeared about ready to say more, when she heard a noise upstairs. "I must get up there and see Mother. She may need something."

"I'll get out of your way, but if there's anything I can do please tell me."

"Thank you, Ernest. I'll let you know."

"I can let myself out. You go up to your Mother."

CHAPTER 20

Ernest returned to his home after leaving Eleanor. He lived in a two-storied farmhouse bequeathed to him by his uncle, who had been a farmer on the west edge of town. He inherited the house and a sizeable barn as well as a multiple bay garage. He had never married and so rattled around a house too large for his needs. He used his living room as a music room where he had a small organ as well as a piano. He ate his meals in the kitchen and relaxed in a small room off the kitchen, which had been used by his aunt for her plants. It was to this room that he retreated after his visit with Eleanor. He customarily spent his Sunday afternoons in this hideaway usually with a book he was reading at the time. Thomas Hardy novels were among his favorites.

It had begun to rain as he returned to his house after visiting with Eleanor. On this particular Sunday afternoon, Ernest settled into his easy chair and took up *Return of the Native* and began re-reading his favorite. But he soon found his mind wandering. Leaving Hardy's *native* to his experiences upon his return to his home, he began pondering Eleanor's homecoming. Sadly hers had been a homecoming to find both her father and mother gone. He felt sure that there was more she had wanted to tell him. He determined to find a way to give her that chance. The more he thought about Eleanor's situation, the more he realized that the only way to help her, if possible, would be to go to her house and see if she would be willing to visit some more. *It would have to be today. I've got a couple of mechanic jobs tomorrow and piano lessons after school.*

Ernest's experience with women had been limited until lately. Mostly older women in the church and mothers of his piano students. But he had recently begun dating Emily whom he had come to know at the church.

And now, what a coincidence to have found Emily's sister. There was certainly nothing romantic about his consideration of Eleanor—just a person whose need for a friend had become evident to him.

After Ernest left, Eleanor went up to her mother and cared for some of her routine needs. Her mother soon fell asleep again. Eleanor stayed in a rocking chair beside her mother's bed. Outside her window the clouds had turned dark gray and it had begun to rain. As the smell of fresh rain filtered through a narrow opening in the window, Eleanor was transported back to rainy days in her childhood, playing with her dolls in this very room and upon the oval rag rug under her rocker. This was a heavy rain pelting her window, unlike the light misty rains she had experienced in Illinois City

Things were so different back here in Iowa. The rain. The bigger trees. Just a feeling of familiarity. The sense of belonging, which she had never felt in Montana, and certainly not in Chicago. Until Landi came into her life. She had felt so "at home" with him. *Even when he was away on one of his trucking jobs. He would always soon be back. Almost like we were already a married couple. But now he's gone from my life—forever.*

Here in Iowa, though it was her home, she still felt a vague unrest, a nameless anxiety, which clouded what could have been a joy of having returned to her roots. She couldn't put her finger on her feeling. Perhaps it was, at least in part, the resentment which she knew her sister felt toward her. Most obviously her father's death and her mother's mental departure had struck her with sorrowful shock. Nothing to do but to sit here and offer her mother small comforts. Worst of all she had lost her chance to reconnect with her parents. More deeply than that, to *reconcile.* She felt so alone. Ever since leaving on that first fateful bus ride—until Landi came, but now he was gone.

She thought of Ernest and his seemingly sincere interest in her feelings. Interrupted by her mother's needs, she had wanted to share more of her feelings with him. She found herself wishing she could talk further with him.

A sudden thunder clap kept her from hearing the door bell, as well as caused her mother to stir. When sleep returned something made her want to check downstairs. The rain had increased in intensity, keeping Ernest from running back to his car. When Eleanor looked out, however he was walking down the porch steps. She quickly opened the door and called. "Ernest. I didn't hear you."

He turned around. "I rang, but I figured you must be involved with your Mom."

"No, she's sleeping. Please come back in."

He came up the steps and explained, "Eleanor, I just couldn't get it out of my mind that there was more you wanted to tell me. . . I hope you don't mind."

"Oh, no. I'm glad you've come back." She held the door for him as he entered the house. "Why don't we go back into the kitchen? I'll make us a pot of tea. OK?"

Ernest sat quietly at the table while Eleanor prepared the tea. She felt something about Ernest that made her not only willing but eager to share her story with him. She brought a pot and two cups to the table and sat down opposite her visitor.

"Let me start at the beginning of my saga. When I graduated from high school here I went to work at Schaeffer's. It was a menial job on the bottom rung. I soon became bored. I could just see myself getting stuck here in this little berg, as I thought of it then. So I decided to bolt–to go up to Chicago. I dreamed of getting a really good job there with lots of income, an apartment of my own and lots of new friends. And a future. Not like here. It would be better in Chicago, I said to myself.

"Well, it wasn't. In fact--worse. A lousy two-bit job in a place that had some pretty unsavory activities going on upstairs. A seedy place to live. And no friends."

"Then, you came back to Iowa?"

"Oh no, not me. I chased my dream to the West. I heard about gold mines in Montana and decided that was where I wanted to go. So I did. That turned out to be another dumb idea. So here I am back where I started." Something kept her from saying anything about Landi.

"Did you keep in touch with your parents during all that time?"

"No. . . and that's what really hurts" Tears began to streak down her face.

"I'm sorry, Eleanor. Because your folks are gone from you?"

"Yes." She wiped her eyes with a paper napkin. "And my sister, too."

"Oh? How so?" He had a strange look about him.

"She's angry with me because I left, forsaking my part of the responsibility for our parents and for this house." She pondered her reply. "Which I did.. . . . without knowing it. Do you know Emily?"

"As a matter of fact, I do. We first met back in high school." He hesitated and then, "And lately we have been dating . . ."

"You have?"

"Well, yes. In fact we are going out Friday."

Eleanor looked surprised, but continued her story. "I'm helping as much as I can with Mother, and in that way I am relieving Emily, and in that way I am trying to make it up to her."

"I'm sorry you two are at odds."

"Yeah. . . but my real problem is me. I feel so guilty for letting my parents down, that I left them and didn't show any love for them by not keeping in touch.

"I told myself that I would write them after things got better for me. I guess I had the feeling that I had to prove myself right to get a good job and a successful future before contacting them. That didn't happen in Chicago. . . anything but that. And then in Montana it didn't pan out either. So I came back here, and found out I was too late." With that she began to weep. "I didn't belong in Chicago, or in Montana, and now I don't belong here either."

"You belong here. This will always be your home, I should think, Eleanor."

"I thought I could cozy up in this nice old house like I did growing up. Not so! Father is gone. Mother is a stranger. Emily rejects me."

Not knowing what to say about Emily's feeling, Ernest asked. "How did you feel about Montana?"

"It's beautiful, but the jobs didn't work out for me. But Iowa is where I am and I don't know what's to come of me."

"I'm sorry."

Then she said something which later she would regret. "Then when I met you, I thought maybe. . . we might. . . have something. . . but you belong to Emily."

Ernest was openly embarrassed when he heard Eleanor's declaration, and didn't know how to respond. He looked at his watch and declared that he needed to get back to a project he had going at home.

After walking Ernest to the door, Eleanor went into the parlor just off the entry hall and sat down. The family rarely used this room reserved for formal visits with strangers. *This is where I belong—a stranger in this house. I feel trapped here. . . while Mother lingers. . . .* But it would not be for long.

CHAPTER 21

A week later Eleanor sat in the front pew of St. John's church feeling very much alone, even though Emily was seated a few spaces down the same pew. Immediately in front of Eleanor was her mother's closed casket with spray of flowers on its cover. The pastor was a man in his forties, apparently new to St. John's, perhaps two or three years. Ernest was at the organ, poised to play the final hymn after the pastor's eulogy. Eleanor found the pastor's words to be quite comforting, but at the same time she was unable to let go of her feeling that she had let he mother down and had alienated herself from her sister.

After the service, she and Emily were ushered into the mortician's limousine. They rode in silence to the cemetery for the interment. On the return trip, also in silence, Eleanor and Emily returned to the church for the reception in the basement. The reception was something to be endured and as soon as she felt she could escape, Eleanor returned to the Anthes hotel. She did not want to be alone in her room. So she entered the hotel coffee shop in which she chose a booth to sit and think. She was profoundly disturbed by something the pastor had said. "As our loved ones live on in our memories, they provide us a foretaste of heaven when we will be given the high privilege of re-joining them for eternity." *High privilege–huh! I feel so bad about how I treated them, that I'm scared to see them again–even if that were possible.*

Just then someone came to her booth. "May I join you?"

She looked up to see Ernie."Why, yes, I guess so. . . But. . . ."

"But, what?"

"What will my sister think?"

"You mean, because we are dating?"

"Yes."

"She encouraged me to see you."

"She did!"

"She's worried about you, Eleanor." With that he entered the booth and sat opposite Eleanor before continuing. "For one thing, she says you are so different after coming back."

"How so? I wonder."

"I don't exactly know, but the one word she used was *hardened.* You seem to her hardened to life, not the innocent girl you used to be."

"I'll have to think about that. . . ."

"And then she wonders what you will do. If you'll stay in town. If so, where will you live, and what will you do."

At this point the waitress came to the booth and asked Ernest what he wanted to order.

"Just coffee."

Eleanor was obviously bewildered by what she had been told.

"Eleanor, I am saddened that Emily and you haven't been able to talk about this stuff."

"I know. It is awful." Not wanting to discuss the matter, she asked Ernest. "Has this always been your home town?"

"I grew up here and graduated from high school the same year as Emily. Then after I worked at the Ford garage I went out on my own in the car repair business. My parents are both gone, so I live alone in the home place. . . the way it will be for Emily now."

"So organ playing is your other interest, then?"

"Yes, but in some ways my real passion is antique auto restoration. In fact, I have been working on a couple of your father's cars in the garage behind the house on Avenue I."

"Is that right! I'd like to see that sometime."

"I'd be glad to show you sometime." He finished the last bit of his coffee. "But, now I need to be running along." With that, he rose to leave the booth "Good bye. Nice talking to you."

"Thanks." Eleanor ordered a re-fill and remained with a lot to think about, with what Ernest had said.. About Emily's observation that she had become hardened. *Chicago did that to me—not only my experience but Landi's. And Illinois City and Missoula in a way as well. Certainly saw another side of life from the innocent life here at home. Even the way I left home and didn't write had a hardening effect upon me, I suppose.*

Guilt and remorse took over her consciousness as she finished her coffee and got up to leave the café and to go upstairs to her hotel room. She took her place in a chair beside the window and next to her bed. There she remained motionless for an hour or so as she contemplated her situation. Heartsick over the past and her failure, and now deeply perplexed over what was ahead for her life. Her loss of relationship with her family loomed ever-present in her mind as she thought about the future.

Her room phone rang and reached over o the bed-side table to answer it. "Hello."

"Hello, Eleanor. This is Ernest."

Surprised she replied, "Oh, Ernest. . . ."

"I've been concerned about how you are feeling about things, and I really wonder if you ought to try and have a visit with Pastor Bieler."

"Oh, I don't know. . . ."

"I've heard that he is really good at helping people sort through their problems."

"I hardly know him."

"That's no problem. . . In fact, I would like to take you over to the church and I'll introduce you to him. . . How about I pick you up on Monday morning and we'll go over to St. John's? I'll phone him for an appointment—OK?"

"If you really think he can help me."

"Good. I'll let you know what time."

The following Monday, Ernest came by for Eleanor in a dark blue Dodge coupe. "Ths is one of the cars I've been working on in the Avenue 'I' shop."

"I like it. It's cute."

Eleanor found it easy to talk with Pastor Bieler after Ernest had provided a preliminary introduction and then left the two in the pastor's study. He had asked her to share a brief run-down of her life to date-- where she had lived and what she had worked at—things like that.

He then asked, "What is it that brings you here, Eleanor? What troubles you?"

She seemed to question what she should say. He interjected. "Of course, I know that losing your mother must be heavy on your heart."

"Yes, but I had lost her before I returned, with her consciousness having been shut down, making it impossible for me to communicate with her. And Father had died before I returned. That hit me hard."

"When was the last time you and your parents had contact through letters or phone calls?"

Obviously agitated, she answered, "That's just it. Not since I left for Chicago."

"How long ago was that?"

"About three years."

"How do you feel about that?"

"Quite badly."

"Is that something you want to talk about?"

"No. . . not now anyway." She changed the subject. "And another thing. I've lost Emily as well, the way she has avoided me since my return. She told Ernest that I seem so hardened. . . whatever that means."

Eleanor and Pastor Bieler spent a considerable amount of time discussing these issues on Eleanor's mind and heart.

Realizing it was time to conclude this first session, Pastor Bieler offered, "You have gone through a lot of troubling times and it is no wonder you have things that bother you. We need to stop at this point, but if you'd like to come back we can take up some of these matters which you may want to discuss further. Would you want to come again, Eleanor?"

"Yes, I guess so."

"Good. Same time next Tuesday?"

"O.K."

On the next Monday morning, Eleanor was surprised by a phone call from Emily. "Hello, Eleanor. This is Emily."

"Why, hello!"

"Mother's lawyer has asked you and me to come to his office this afternoon for the reading of the will at two o'clock. Ernest is taking me, and we can pick you up at quarter to. Would that be OK?" She spoke in a very business-like manner, leaving Eleanor wondering what kind of a session it would be with the lawyer.

"Yes, I will be waiting for you in the lobby."

"Good, we will see you then."

Eleanor thought to herself after Emily hung up, *I never even thought about a will. I assumed there is nothing much left with all the care which both my parents needed at the end. Maybe the house, but that would be about all. Father was always quite closed-mouthed about finances, so I really have no idea what to expect. And I assume it will all go to Emily.*

In Ernest's car on the way to the attorney's office, Emily did not say a word. She appeared glum. Ernest tried to keep a bit of conversation going but to everyone's relief they reached the office by two o'clock.

The receptionist ushered them into a small conference room and showed them to their seats at the table. Emily positioned herself in such a way that she did not have to look a Eleanor. The receptionist asked if anyone would like coffee. They declined.

After five minutes or so, the lawyer entered the room and offered his condolences. He then introduced himself. "I'm Harold Kohler. I have been your parents attorney for many years And it now is my task to take care of their final wishes."

He took out a sheaf of paper and announced. "I have here the last will and testament of your mother, Cora Helm which I drew up according to her wishes a few weeks before she slipped into a coma. While your father's will left the entire estate to his wife, he had confided in me his wishes regarding the disposition of the estate upon Cora's death. I shared his wishes with Mrs. Helm and her will then follows his wishes as well . . . with one exception." Mr. Kohler paused and then offered subsequent information. "I would like to read Mr. Helm's letter of intent which he left for Mrs. Helm after his death. It is as follows:

> *"Dear Cora,*
> *I would like for you to consider bequeathing $2,000 to Eleanor; my garage, and its contents, including the 1927 Nash, and the property upon which it is built to Ernest Hauser; and our house together with its entire contents to Emily; and finally the full balance of my assets to Emily.*
> *Your loving husband*

The attorney paused to let the full impact of Mr. Helm's wishes register. Ernie's expression showed complete surprise. Emily's expression was one of satisfaction, while Eleanor looked perplexed.

Mr. Kohler then read Mrs. Helm's will, which as he had indicated, followed her husband's wishes with two exceptions.

> *I bequeath $2,000, or the balance in my checking account, whichever is smaller, to Eleanor; my garage, and its contents including the 1927 Nash, and the property upon which it is built to Ernest Hauser; our house on Avenue I, and the real property on which it is built to Eleanor, and the contents of our house to Emily, and finally the full balance of my other assets to Emily*

The attorney then added, "I should also point one additional qualification which Cora placed upon the cash designated for Eleanor, that referring to her checking account at the time of death. In that regard I should inform you that the balance at the time of her death was $898. The estimated value of the remaining assets is somewhere upward from fifty thousand, and you should not count on a final distribution for another nine to 12 months."

The three intended recipients of Cora's estate were quiet and this time unexpressive.

"Are there any questions?"

No one had any questions at this point

"Then, if you will excuse me, I will depart and you can remain as long as you want to. My office will inform you as to next steps when they are to be taken."

After Kohler left, the room was silent. Ernest was the first to comment. "I am totally surprised about the garage and car, but I have to admit that it will be a wonderful place for me to carry on my old car hobby."

"I am really glad for you," Eleanor responded. Then after a pause. "So far as the $898 and the house, I don't deserve either of those."

"Then that would leave you with zero," Emily commented.

"That's right."Ernie broke the silence again. "I need to leave for some other business, but I want both of you to be my guests for dinner tomorrow night at the hotel café. How about it?"

Each of the sisters nodded assent.

"Now, let me take you back to your place, Eleanor, and Emily, come with me, would you?"

All three rose from their seats and awkwardly made their way out. Eleanor was the last to leave the room. As she passed the desk the receptionist handed her an envelope. "Ms. Helm, this is for you."

The next morning Eleanor had her appointment with Rev. Beiler. He began the session, "I've been mulling over what you shared with me last week and I have a couple of questions which keep coming back," Pastor Bieler said as he leaned back in his desk chair. "But, first, what has been going through your mind since we talked?"

She had to think for a few moments. "I guess I have been thinking more about my time in Chicago and in Montana."

"Yes?"

"I realize how lonely I felt in Chicago."

"Can you tell me a little more about your life in Chicago?"

She was very hesitant.

"Where did you live?"

"I found a small furnished apartment on the third floor of a building on West Monroe Avenue, just south of Madison. Most of the other people in the building were families with children, or retired couples. No young singles like me. It was near a corner soda fountain and sandwich shop on Madison where I got a job. It was small and I was usually the only one in the shop, except for the owner who lived upstairs. So I was alone at work and in the evenings in my apartment. . . and there wasn't any other opportunity to meet people my age."

"Quite a contrast from when you lived here, where in this size town we all seem to know a lot of other people."

"That's for sure." She was deep in thought. "I really did not like anything about Chicago. In fact I was repulsed by it." She thought further. "When I left Iowa for Chicago I know now I was seduced by my imagination of the city and its glitter and delights. I thought I'd find a good job and make a lot of money and have a lot of fun. Well, none of that happened. Instead I saw a lot of ugliness and sin. I felt that a lot of that rubbed off on me. That's why I wanted to get away to Montana."

"Was it better there for you?"

"In some ways but I still felt lonely in Illinois City. . . until I got to know Landi."

"What was it about Landi? How did he help you?"

"He didn't boss me around. Sort of accepted me as I was."

"Others had not accepted you before that?"

"Not really."

"Not even your parents?"

She seemed very reluctant to answer. "How about your sister?"

Martin Bieler sat patiently for as long as it took for Eleanor to begin to answer. "Emily looked up to me, but down deep she was quite different from me and I think she didn't understand who I really was. . . now that I think of it. I could not have thought that through at the time."

"That is what talks like this can do for you. This can help you see things now that you didn't see at the time. Your parents?"

After a moment of pondering, "They thought of me as their little girl in little white stockings over my knees, and a tiny frilly pink dress with no shape to the bodice. Certainly not as a young woman struggling to be an adult."

"Struggling?"

"Even as a high school senior, they didn't want me dating boys. I could go to the youth group here at church but that was always in a group, with an adult leader present."

"How did you get along in that group? Did you feel like you were one of the group?"

"Strange that you should ask. The truth is that I always felt like an outsider."

"Can you say why that was?"

Just then an outside door could be heard as it opened and someone came into the sanctuary.

"I think your ride has come and we need to bring this session to a close. But I want you to come in next week and between now and then why don't you think about this question of not being accepted, feeling like you were an outsider. . . . and then the question I have for you to think about as well, is why you did not keep in contact with your family after you left?"

The pastor rose from his chair to see Eleanor out. "Same time next week."

Ernest was waiting inside near the outer doors. "All set? I'll get you back to your hotel."

"Thanks, Ernie." She responded as the two walked out to his car at the curb.

Once in the car he offered, "You look like you could use a cup of tea. Let me get you one in your hotel café."

"You sure?" She said hesitantly.

"Yes, It's alright with Emily, if that's what you are worried about. In fact, she has something she wants me to tell you."

"Oh?"

"When we get our tea I'll tell you."

The waitress brought their tea and Ernest began immediately to share some thoughts her sister had for Eleanor. "Emily wants you to know that you can move into the house on Ave I while you are still in limbo and chatting with Pastor Bieler!"

"What about Emily? Isn't that where she is living?"

"Yes, but she said she is gone so much of the time to work and elsewhere that you can have the back bedroom and bath at the foot of the back stairs. You can come and go on your own." Ernest added his own thought. "The Anthes is going to be too much expense for as long as you may be here."

"I guess you are right. I might as well give that idea a try. Maybe I won't be around that long. I don't know."

"If you want, I can help you move over there right now. You can check out after our tea."

"Alright."

Eleanor went upstairs and packed her few things and came down to check out. Ernie picked up her suitcase and when she paid her bill, they drove to the house on avenue I, where Eleanor moved in.

After Ernest drove away, the house was empty and filled with silence as Eleanor sat down in a rocking chair by the window in the back bedroom —now hers for awhile. Her conversation with Martin Bieler came to the fore in her mind, particularly the word, *accept*. She had never before seen her feeling of the lack of acceptance by others as such an issue in her life. *When I think about it now, I guess there was no one whom I thought really accepted me for who I was.*

Up until now she had not understood what it was about Ernest which struck a chord in her life. Now she could see that it was Ernie's acceptance of her which had been so appealing to her from the day she met him. *The only other person in my life to accept me as I am has been Landi.* For some reason that idea troubled her.

It was more difficult for Eleanor to think about why she had not contacted her family after she had left home. It would take pondering over this matter in the days following, before she had something of an answer.

CHAPTER 22

For her third appointment to talk with the pastor, she found that she could easily walk to the church. When she arrived, Martin Bieler was waiting for her. "Good afternoon, Eleanor."

"Hello. Pastor Bieler."

"Good to see you again, Eleanor. Let's go in and sit down."

When they were seated, Martin asked. "Have you had any thoughts about what we talked about last week?"

"Well, I have concluded that very few people in my life have accepted me as I am, and that has affected how things have turned out for me. . . so far."

"What do you think have been the results of your feeling that others did not accept you?"

"Well, I think it has made me a loner."

"How?"

"I shy away from people. If they don't talk to me, I don't have anything to say to them."

"You say that people don't accept you. Could it be that is because you don't accept them? Perhaps you shy away from people and that puts a distance between you and others, which you interpret as non-acceptance? And could that be why you didn't contact your family after you left to go to Chicago?"

Eleanor was quiet for a prolonged time. Martin waited. Then in a child-like voice, she answered, "Maybe."

"How do you feel about that?"

She was quiet and downcast. "I am overcome with guilt. . . I've hurt my parents. . . And now they are gone. . . and I can't make it right." She began to sob. Through her tears she haltingly said, "And. . . I'll have to . . . live with. . . it. . . ."

"With what?"

". . . This terrible guilt."

"I would like to help you with your feeling of guilt. I want you to write down during the next week, word for word, what you wish you could have said to your mother and your father. Then, would you bring your written statements with you next week. I will not read them. They are yours alone, but I'd like to help you handle your feelings. And also, please bring with you a photo of your parents."

"I'll do that."

Then Pastor Bieler added, "And Eleanor, there is one other aspect of your thinking which I'd like to address. We have talked about the connection between your accepting other people and their accepting you. How do you see that relationship of acceptances?"

Eleanor thought for a moment. "That when I accept others, I'll find that they accept me."

"That's right. And the thing that keeps you from accepting others and thinking that they don't accept you is that you have trouble accepting yourself and believing that you are really okay."

Eleanor thought about this for a while. "I think I see what you mean, Pastor."

"Good. And when you come to feel that God loves you as you are, all these other acceptances begin to work out better for you . . . Now I'm preaching, but think about it, Eleanor, will you?"

"I will."

"That's all for today. Be sure to bring your written statement and pictures of your parents next time."

Eleanor left the church and began her walk home. She thought again about the note her mother had left for her which she was given after the meeting with the lawyer. On that day as soon she had returned to the privacy of her room, she had read the note.

> *Dear Eleanor,*
>
> *My reason for giving the house to you was to offer you the opportunity to return home after all these years. My hope is that when you return to your childhood house you will want to stay there. If not, it is yours to do with it what you decide.*

Goodbye, Eleanor. I have missed you all these years
My love to you forever.
Mother

After reading this posthumous message from her mother, Eleanor had thrown herself upon her bed and sobbed almost uncontrollably, until she was overcome with sleep. When she awakened, she realized vaguely that she had been with her mother in her comatose condition. In her sleep-induced imagination Eleanor heard her mother say to her. *You're home, child. Now I am happy again.*

In that moment of realization, Eleanor had felt a deep sense of relief. She immediately began to plan how she would approach Emily at an appropriate time.

Now as she walked back to "her" house on Avenue "I," she knew that the meal with Emily and Ernie that evening would be a perfect time to declare her intentions.

When Eleanor joined Ernie and Emily for dinner, she had already worked out what she planned to say to them regarding their mother's wishes. In part it had been the message from her mother which had helped her make up her mind.

After the three ate their meal and lingered with their coffee, Eleanor announced, "I have decided to give the house to you, Emily. You have earned it. And you plan to live here, I think."

Emily made an attempt to dissuade her sister. "If Mother wanted you to have the house, then you should."

"No, I am sure now that it would be alright with her for me to give it to you. And I do not plan to remain in Iowa."

At this point Ernest entered the discussion. "Oh? Where do you plan to go?"

"I'm not sure. Possibly Montana. But before leaving, I will ask Mr. Kohler to do the paperwork for deeding the house to you, Emily."

"Eleanor, I will always be grateful to you. I hope you will find what you are looking for in Montana, or wherever you go."

"Yes," Ernie joined in.

"Thank you both." Eleanor was almost in tears.

With that the dinner party came to an end.

For her next appointment, Martin Bieler met her at the door and led Eleanor into the sanctuary and seated her in the front pew. He stood facing her. "Do you have the statements you want to make to your parents?"

"Yes."

"And the photos? May I place them up here on the communion table so that you can see from where you are sitting.?

"Yes. Here they are." She handed Martin the photos and he put them up on the table. Martin then pulled a chair up to the front pew facing Eleanor. "I want to offer you a chance to express yourself to your parents in a very special way. It is a form of prayer. When we pray to God, we are often telling God what is on our hearts, oftentimes these are requests to God. What I want you to do is what I like to call *Heavenly Healing.* In your case, Eleanor, I want to help you heal your relationship with your mother and father, even though they are no longer here with you, but rather are in heaven with God.

"To do this I will lead us in prayer and then ask you to whisper your prayer by reading the messages to your parents which you have written. As you do this, pretend that you are with them in some familiar place in your home. When you have finished say AMEN. Do you understand this procedure?"

"Yes."

Martin then began the prayer. *Oh Lord, we acknowledge that your children, Eleanor's, mother and father, are safely and happily at home with you in your heavenly kingdom. Hear her prayer-message to them now as Eleanor offers her heartfelt thoughts in her whispered prayer.*

Eleanor whispered her message in deep earnest words of contrite love. And then concluded with an audible AMEN. She sat quietly with tears streaming down her face while the pastor gave her long moments of silence before concluding his prayer. *Hear our prayers in the name of Christ who heals all our relationships. Amen.*

After a prolonged period of silence Martin handed Eleanor the photos and an envelope in which she was to seal her written message. "Anything you want to say before you go?"

"I feel as though a ton of bricks has been taken off my chest."

"Good. Is that all?"

"No. You have given me a lot to think about."

With that, her sessions with Martin Bieler came to an end.

When Eleanor entered the house and went up to her back bedroom, she was overwhelmed with the thought that her parents were no longer here and she herself no longer needed to be here in Emily's house.

The next day Eleanor made an appointment with the family attorney. She asked him to pepare the paperwork for transferring the ownership of the house to Emily when that aspect of the estate settlement came up for processing. She told the attorney that she intended to vacate the house personally and that she planned to move away.

Upon hearing her plans, Harold Kohler had his secretary issue her a check for the $898. "You might as well have this now instead of waiting until all has been settled."

Later that day Emily and Ernest came to the house to talk with Eleanor. Before they were able to share with her their news. Eleanor announced to them, "I plan to leave town in a day or two."

"Oh! Where do you plan to go?"

"Montana."

Ernie and Emily looked at each other conspiratorially. Then Emily blurted out,

"Why?"

Ernie answered, "Well we haven't told you, but we plan to be married next Saturday."

"And we want you to be there," Emily said. "In fact I would like you to be my maid of honor. It will be just a small ceremony . . . Mother's death and all . . . Would you?"

"Oh, Emily, I would love to."

The next Saturday Eleanor stood next to her sister before the altar in St. John's Church. Ernest and his brother from Burlington stood next to them facing Pastor Bieler.

In the months following, Eleanor would not remember much of what was said in the ceremony, but she would hold dearly to her heart a new feeling of having been reunited with her family.

The day after Emily's wedding, the bus pulled away from the curb to begin its way to the highway. Ernie and Emily watched and waved. Emily threw a kiss, and then turned to leave with Ernie as the bus disappeared from view. Peering out her window seat, a tear rolled down Eleanor's cheek, not so much from guilt and regret as from bittersweet joy. . . anxious eagerness as well.. . about to enter an unknown chapter. Unknown in more ways than one. But the strange part was that she felt she would now be able to conduct her own life free of the feelings or expectations of others.

CHAPTER 23

Arriving in Chicago at the bus terminal, Eleanor found a taxi and instructed the cab driver, "The station where I can get the Northern Pacific Railroad train?"

"Yes Ma'm," the Cabby responded as he began a short drive from the downtown bus terminal to Union Station. When they arrived, he got her suitcase and handed it to her as she got out onto the sidewalk. After paying the driver, she walked into the station and headed for one of the ticket windows. She peered into the window at the agent who greeted her. "May I help you?"

"Yes, what is the first town of some size as you get into Montana?"

"That would be Miles City–or better yet–Billings. It's one of the largest cities in Montana."

"I'd like a ticket to Billings, then."

"Round trip?"

"No, just one way."

He sold her the ticket and then warned, "You better get over to track 10. She's almost ready to leave." He pointed her to the direction of boarding trains.

"Thank you very much." She took hold of her two suitcases and rushed through the large cavernous waiting room to the gate which announced: *Northern Pacific–BILLINGS, MONTANA*. She went through the gate and out onto the cement walk under the canopy. Ahead of her as she walked she saw the club car of the train to her right along the cement platform. She followed a line of other passengers about to board.

A porter helped her up the steps into the nearest coach just as the conductor called out ***"All aboard."***

She found an empty seat by a window and put her suitcases on the rack above, and then settled down as the train began to roll. Soon a conductor came through the car and punched her ticket. She relaxed and began peering out her window. First the small factories and tall tenements passed by, then the small frame houses, and trees along the streets. It wasn't long before farms and crop lands began to appear. *Here I go again,* she said to herself before turning her thoughts inward. *I'm a different person now. Last time I was running away from home, from my parents and from Chicago and the Mob. And, I guess, running away from myself! Now's when I make a new, clean start. I'm running to something this time. But to what?*

Over the previous few weeks Eleanor had frequently sighed in relief as she thought about the lifting of her guilt over having left her parents. But what troubled her now was, *What's ahead for me?*

Once again Eleanor Helm was headed out into the unknown without a job or a place to live, having cut her ties to the past. The first time was Chicago and the second Montana. Now Montana yet again. This time she had no unresolved ties to Iowa. Nor in Montana either. *And I feel so alone* now that Landi was gone and presumably dead. *Landi—how different my life would have been had he not been gunned down by the Mob. He could have established his ow trucking business. We could have married and lived in a little house with our children and pets. A picket fence. . .a yard. . .and a garden. . . and. . .a. . . .* With that she fell asleep as her train rolled west.

She had chosen Billings, concluding that she would have more chance of employment in a larger city. Her surmise would turn out to be correct. That evening, after a long stop in St. Paul the train rolled on into the night. The next morning Eleanor looked out onto the dry plains of eastern Montana. Sometime around midday the train pulled to a stop at Billings. She made her way onto the platform and into the rather extensive waiting room. When she saw that the ticket agent's window was free, she went up to him and asked for directions to a hotel.

"You'll find the Carlin Hotel across the street and just down a block or two."

"Thank you." Eleanor walked out of the depot and onto Montana Avenue, where she had no trouble finding the Carlin which had a vacancy. When she asked about employment opportunities in Billings, the desk clerk asked her what her work experience had been.

"I have done some housekeeping in a hotel in Missoula, but that's about all."

"Let me have you talk to our manager."

To her good fortune, there was a position of linen room manager open, which the manager offered to her. She accepted and started work the next day. Her first few days she was given a room in the Carlin until she could find something suitable. The second morning she met with the four chamber maids under her supervision to become acquainted and organized. When the main business was concluded, she asked, "Do any of you know where I could find an apartment, hopefully not too far from here?"

Joyce, one of the younger women immediately volunteered. "I do. There are a couple of apartments open in the building where I am."

"Good. Where is that, Joyce?"

"I live in The Barbizon, a downtown apartment house dedicated to serving women, keeping them safe. It is just on 29th Street, only about four blocks from here, close enough to walk to work at the Carlin. I'd be glad to take you over there after work."

"I'd appreciate that."

The Barbizon proved to be an excellent accommodation for Eleanor. She found the Belknap Broiler nearby to be a good place to take her meals. A daily routine soon developed with her work days in the Carlin and her evenings and overnights in the Barbizon and at the Belknap Broiler for breakfasts and suppers. Her work was going quite well. She felt that she had exceeded the manager's expectations. However, she could see that there would be no chance of advancement. She had to admit that she was lonely, as well.

One day on her way back to the Barbizon after work, she passed the Northern Hotel, a much larger and more upscale hotel than the Carlin. On impulse she stepped into the ornate lobby and went up to the desk. "Whom may I speak to regarding employment?"

"You need to speak with our Assistant Manager over there in that office." He pointed to an open door. "Just drop in, he'll be glad to talk to you."

"Thank you very much." Eleanor walked over to the Assistant Manager's office.

He greeted her. "How may I help you?"

"Hello. I am Eleanor Helm and I work at the Carlin. I wondered if you might have an opening here for which I might apply."

"Possibly. But first, what makes you want to change?"

Eleanor had anticipated such a question and answered truthfully. "For no negative reason, sir. I think I am doing fine at the Carlin, but I felt that I'd like to be involved in a larger, busier place. Quite frankly I find that there are a lot of down-times, and it is a lonely job at such times. . . and I thought the pay might be a bit higher here, though that is not the basic reason."

"Well, I like your honesty. I'll have you fill out this application and then I will let you know if something opens which I think you could fill." He handed her an application form on a clipboard for her to complete while she remained seated in his office.

After she filled it out, she gave it to him and he said. "I'll let you know, Miss Helm."

It was a couple of weeks before she got a call from the Northern offering a job at the desk for the late afternoon to late night hours. This was the period during with most of the check-ins, making it the busiest of the three eight-hour shifts. Eleanor accepted the offer and began the following Monday afternoon.

Eventually her resources were such that she could buy a house of her own on Lewis Avenue not far from the Northern. After so many unfortunate moves in her life, Billings would become her permanent home. Nothing too exciting one way or the other. She was one of a growing number of single women working in downtown Billings and living not too far away in a quiet residential neighborhood. She had a vegetable and flower garden in the summer time and enjoyed a quilting group in her church in the winter time. This group provided her with friends with whom she occasionally went on outings of one sort or another. She had joined First Congregational Church a couple of blocks away from the Northern. By and large life was good, but she still had to admit that she was lonely. No one like Ernie had appeared, and certainly there was no Landi in her life, a condition she had more or less come to terms with.

Her work at the hotel became her passion. She found herself fascinated with the hotel business. In time she was surprised when Carl Holbrook, her manager, called her into his office one morning.

"Miss Helm. Please sit down for a moment. I have a proposal to make." He held the seat In front of his desk for her.

"Thank you, Mr. Holbrook."

"I have been impressed with your work at the desk, not only in your dealing with guests, but with your understanding of the business side of the Northern. As perhaps you know, my assistant is moving on to take a position in a Chicago hotel at the end of the month. Instead of advertising this position here, I would like to ask you first if you would be interested in moving up to assistant manager?"

"Why, yes, I believe I would, as long as you think I can fill that role." Eleanor answered without hesitation.

"That's what I hoped you would say."

"Thank you."

"Give me a few days to fill your desk position and then we'll get you started in the assistant's office. . . and by the way, after that its not Mr. Holbrook–it will be Carl."

In two week's time, Eleanor Helm was the new assistant manager of the Northern Hotel, a position she would hold for a little over a year, when she received a phone call from Carl's wife.

"Hello, Miss Helm. this is Mrs. Holbrook, I am sorry to tell you that last night Carl had a heart attack and he is in Deaconess Hospital in Intensive Care. He would like for you to see him for some instructions, I presume."

"I'm so sorry. I will go right up."

When Eleanor stepped into his room, she found Carl awake and sitting up slightly, but with more tubes and wires connected to him than she could count. "Carl, how are you?"

"Not the best, but I don't know yet, what is ahead for me. That's why I needed to talk to you." He paused to get his breath.

"Yes?"

"I want you to take over as manager until I get out of here. . . but just in case! You should contact the owners and tell them what is going on with me. And then, I guess keep them informed."

"I'll do that . ."

At that point a nurse came in and Eleanor made her exit.

A week later Carl died on the operating table. The owners immediately contacted Eleanor and asked her to assume the full position of manager, which she accepted.

PART III

Separation

CHAPTER 24

About 20 miles from Naples on the west coast of Italy lies Castelamarre di Stabia, a little town, a popular destination for tourists. It was in January of 1948 when an American of Italian descent and his wife from Chicago checked into the La Medusa Grand Hotel. He signed in as Sonny and Ruth Casey. In so doing, he discreetly used his wife's maiden name. Ostensibly their visit to Castelamarre was for touring its historic sights and enjoying its seaside delights. Observing that he was quite hard of hearing, the desk clerk addressed Mrs. Casey to tell of the things to see and do during their three-day visit

After the bellman took the American couple to their room, the clerk was struck by a sense of vague recognition. As he thought about it he concluded that, there seemed to be something familiar about the man's unusually round face and puffy cheeks. The name" Sonny" was unusual, but also strangely reminiscent.

Upstairs in their room, Ruth pulled down the bed spread and sheet. "Oh, Albert I want to take a bit of nap before dinner. The trip has tired me." She began to step out of her dress and slip.

"That's OK. But I want to go down and have a look around a bit. I'll be back in an hour or so."

He returned to the lobby and walked around, noticing the name of the clerk on a small plate on the desk. ***L. FERRINI***. *Well I'll be; the very person I am looking for!* After he noticed that the clerk was free of guests, he stepped up. "Mr. Ferrini, I'd like to speak with you privately. Is there a time when we can meet?"

The clerk was wary when he responded, "Right now is fine."

"No, I mean away from your work."

"Well, we could meet over there in the easy chairs in the corner of the lobby. . . in about ten minutes."

"Good, I'll be there." He replied and went over immediately, took a newspaper from a stand and sat down to wait. In a few minutes Ferrini came over and sat down near the American.

Mr. Casey began somewhat tentatively. "Mr. Ferrini, are you by any chance from Chicago?"

The clerk tried to hide his fear laden shock. "What makes you think so?"

"I hear it in your voice. You have a Midwestern accent mixed with Italian."

"Well, as a matter of fact, I have lived in Chicago. A while ago-- before the war. After that–Montana. When the war ended and Americans could travel to Italy again, I moved back here to where my family roots are."

"Yes. Now don't be fearful when I tell you that my real name is Capone."

Ferini went rigid for a moment.

"My father, Al, died in prison on January 25th, 1947. Let me assure you that I am not involved in the Mob, or any illegal activity. I have always been straight. One thug in the family was enough. . . more than enough." He paused. "I am aware that Landino Ferrini was wanted by the Mob and that you fled. Am I right?"

Landino replied reluctantly, "Yes, you are correct."

"And all that is over. You are not, NOT on their list. I am here on my own to give you that assurance. There is little I can do to make amends for what Big Al did over the years. But this much I can do for you, sir."

Landi was quiet for a few moments as he took all this in. "I am most grateful to you, Mr. Casey. . ." Reluctant to let matters drop at this point and a bit wary, he asked, "What brings you to Italy, sir?"

"What did you ask? I'm partially deaf from a childhood infection."

Landi repeated his question more loudly.

"Oh, I came partly to find you, and also to locate the house where my grandparents lived before coming to America. My grandfather had been a barber in Naples."

"Did you find the house?"

"Only the remains of his shop."

"I see, but how did you know I was over here?"

"I was lucky. The innkeeper where we stayed found your name in a directory of hotels in the area."

Landi remained only partially convinced and wanted more of a chance to spot any hint of duplicity in young Capone. "As one-old time Chicagoan to another, I'd like to invite you and Mrs. Casey to dinner this evening. Would you be my guest?"

"We would be glad to, Mr. Ferrini."

"At seven, then? Here in the dining room."

With that the two men parted.

When Sonny returned to the room, he told his wife, Diana, "I told Landino that he was off the hook after Dad died, but I don't think he trusted me. I'm not surprised. Those guys lived in a culture of mistrust and fear."

"You might share more of your own life story. How you grew up clean. Tell him about the famous birthday party."

"Yeah, guess I could do that. He invited us for dinner downstairs tonight at seven."

"That's nice."

Over dinner the three enjoyed an easy conversation emerging as they got to know one another. Landi had started things off when he asked young Capone, "What was it like growing up as a son of Chicago's most notorious mobster? If you don't mind my being blunt about it?"

"Oh, no. That's fine. My father kept his business and his family completely separate. I only had a vague idea of what went on. There was one driver who took us around the city with whom I got acquainted, and he told me some things. Especially when I got older, he and I became friends, and it is through him that I have come to know that they no longer are interested in you."

"What was his name? I might have known him."

"That's one thing he would not divulge. He never let me know his real name. I think it was his way of covering his tracks in case they found out that he had told me stuff."

Diana interjected, "Tell about the birthday party."

"For my 10th birthday, Mother and Dad threw a big party for me. Invited all my friends from Catholic school. They invited fifty kids. Can you believe it?"

"Did that many come?"

"Almost. And he made the parents sign permission slips. I don't exactly know why, but I think it was to make sure the authorities would think it was all on the up and up."

"Did you have that many friends?"

"Not exactly. A lot of them came, I think, because everyone was curious about the Capones. . . . Anyway, my upbringing was straight. My mother said to me many times: 'Don't do as your father did, he broke my heart.'"

After some serious thought, Landi said. "Sonny, I think you can understand that at first I had to be cautious about believing you, lest I walk into a fatal trap. But, now I am inclined to believe that you are honest in assuring me that I am no longer wanted by the Mob."

"You are absolutely right. You are free and clear. In fact, if you have any desire to return to the States, you will be perfectly safe. Let me assure you."

"I am grateful to you for coming all this way to give me that emotional release. Now, let's order dessert."

CHAPTER 25

Billings, Montana–1948

Just off the lobby, not far from the reception desk, was a door with the brass plate announcing: MANAGER. On the desk inside the office the name plate read: *Eleanor Helm*.

In front of the desk were two easy chairs facing each other. One occupied at the moment by a young man in his twenties. The manager sat in the other. The young man was dressed in a white shirt which contrasted with his off-white complexion. The young man's black tie matched his slightly wavy black hair. He had given the manager his name: "Dante Marino." Miss Helm wore a trim blazer of plum color over a white blouse. Her straight skirt was black. She sat at ease with her legs crossed which were surprisingly trim for a woman of perhaps fifty with attractively done gray hair.

"Tell me a bit about yourself, Dante," she said, holding his job application on her lap. She liked to do interviews in an informal sort of way asking about life histories.

"Please call me *Dan*. I was born in western Montana where my parents have a bing cherry orchard on Flathead Lake. They came to America from Italy and settled south of Bigfork where they worked for a cherry producer. Eventually they bought him out, about the time I was born."

"That's interesting." The manager looked at the application and then asked, "I see you would like to take the job opening we have for a night clerk, which you should know involves bookkeeping–doing the accounting from the day's business. Have you had any bookkeeping experience?"

"Yes, I did some of that work for the Finlen in Butte for two summers between my college courses at the School of Mines."

"Your home is up on the Flathead. You were in school in Butte. What brings you to Billings, Dan?"

A little embarrassed, he replied. "My girlfriend, fiancee' that is, lives here. It's where she grew up. We met at the School of Mines. She was in geology and has a job with a geological firm here in Billings."

"I can see why you'd like settle here into a job. When do you plan to be married?"

"Actually as soon as we can. But I thought I'd better get a job first."

Eleanor reviewed a letter of recommendation from the Finlen which Dan had included with his application. "Your application looks good, Dan. The job is yours if you want it."

"I'll take it."

"Good. Come in tomorrow evening at 11 and our other night clerk will brief you."

After the young man left, Ellie had a lot to think about. In a strange way Dan reminded her of Landi. She thought about her days in western Montana many years earlier. *Not good days. Never got anywhere. Always stuck on the bottom rung as a housekeeper. . . But there was Landi. He was going to get me out of there and we would own our own hotel some day. . . But then that dark cloud over his life took him away from me. The mob put him down, like they did to anyone they wanted to silence.* These thoughts brought tears to Ellie's eyes as they always did. She reached into the neck of her dress and fingered the ring on the tiny chain. *I loved him so much that I could never love another. His murder has left me alone with only a shred of hope for my future. . . and now I am still alone. It was just a stroke of luck that I'm back here in Montana,. . . and managing the best hotel in Billings at that..*

In her reverie she often concluded with a lament and a hope. *But there's gotta be more in life. . . . I guess I need another stroke of luck.* Little could she have ever imagined that hiring Dan might turn out to be that stroke of luck.

CHAPTER 26

Not far from the La Medusa Grand Hotel in Cassamarre di Stabia, Landino Ferrini entered through the iron gate into the walled court yard in front of his small house. His shift at the hotel was over in time for him to prepare a supper for himself and Maria Olivia, his cat, whose dignified greeting merited a friendly petting on her furry neck. "Ah! You are glad to see me, Livia! I will fix us some supper soon." This announcement was noted with a generous rubbing against his trousers. Thus Landino's nightly ritual began. "How about some Scampi Fritti? Maria Olivia seemed not to hear. "You like prawns. . . right?" he said, stooping to give her another pet. This time she waved her tail. "Good, then scampi it will be."

The evening sun filled the court yard as the man and his cat finished their supper. Olivia was licking off the remains while Landi settled into his out door rocker. He took up his latest paperback of a story set in Chicago. It had just arrived from his bookseller in Chicago. He looked down at his friend. "Another Chicago story, Liv." She gave him a slight twitch of the tail and went back to her washing in preparation for her evening nap.

When it became too dark to read any longer, he closed the book and thought to himself about Chicago and about the U.S. If he was honest, he would have to say that he missed it, and would go back if he could. He thought of Casey and his assurance that he need have no fear of returning. But would he get enough money, and what about Maria Olivia? You can't take pets overseas, very well. Furthermore, what would he do when he got to America again. But on the other hand there was nothing here in Castellmarre to keep him in Italy. None of his family was left. His cousin, Maria and her husband. *I'd really like to go to Montana. . . to Missoula. . . to see where Ellie's hotel once was . . . .*

He put the matter out of his head, scooped up Livia and they went into the house and to bed. The cat to her pile of blankets on the floor and Landi to his lonely bed.

Just as sleep was beginning to overcome Landi, he heard a fire truck siren in the distance. A shiver went through his body. In the night the sound returned to haunt him in his dreams. He could feel the heat, causing him to sweat and throw off his blankets. Flames were leaping out of third floor windows of a building engulfed in smoke. He was jarred awake by the panicked screams of a woman. Her screams subsided suddenly and Landi was sitting up in his bed. *Eleanor!* He sobbed.. Then as he finally pulled his covers up over him, a strange thing happened. He seemed to hear a familiar voice. *I'm alive, Landi. Come to me.* Olivia meowed. It was as if the cat had heard the voice too. *Or did she?* Landi was a long time going back to sleep. And then only briefly. The next morning Landi could not make any sense out of his dream or the "voice" which followed. He "knew" full well that Eleanor had been a victim of the fire in Missoula. And yet, what had transpired in the night seemed to say that she was still alive *Could that be? If so, I need to find her. But how?*

However, by the time he had had his breakfast and gone to work, he became involved in the routine responsibilities of the work day, the memory of his dream and of Eleanor's *message* had receded from his thinking.

Landi's cousin Maria, and her husband Eduardo lived in his neighborhood. He had become quite involved with Maria and Eduardo and their commercial olive grove, since his return to Italy. It was a few days after his disturbing dream when Landi received a frantic phone call from Maria. "Landi! There has been a terrible accident. Eduardo has been killed when his truck was hit by another vehicle"

"Maria. That's awful. Where are you?"

"At home."

"I'll be right over."

"Oh, thank you!" She hung up and continued to sob.

Landi immediately asked the manager to take over so that he could go to his cousin. He arrived at Maria's and joined a cluster of neighbors who had come to give comfort to his cousin. In the days following, Landi spent all his free time helping Maria with her work in the olive grove.

She worried about what would happen to her olive grove and spoke with Landi about what she should do. It would be a while before she and Landi could come to some conclusion about the future of the family business.

And it would be a while before thoughts of Eleanor's "dream message" would re-surface in Landi' consciousness.

CHAPTER 27

About a year after Dan Marino started work at the desk of the Northern, Eleanor Helm was pleasantly surprised to find this invitation in her mail box:

Mr. and Mrs. Charles Willis
request the honor of your presence
at the marriage of their daughter
Barbara Anne
to
Mr. Dante Joseph Marino
on Saturday, the eighth of June
One thousand, nine hundred and forty seven
a two o'clock in the afternoon
First Congregational Church
310 North 27th Street
Billings, Montana

Over the months during which Eleanor had mentored Dan in the work of the desk clerk and also in the hotel business in general, her feelings for Dan bordered on that of a parent of an adult child. Dan had responded with sincere appreciation and with a growing sense of friendship. In truth this friendship filled some of Eleanor's emptiness. In a strange way it was the vague resemblance of Landi in Dan's personality which drew her to Dan. Not, however, in a romantic way. She had had opportunity on a couple of occasions to meet Barbara Willis, whom she liked from the start. And so it was with a great deal of happy anticipation that Eleanor looked forward to Dan and Barbara's wedding.

June eighth arrived and Dan and Barbara's wedding was everything they had hoped for. Eleanor was thrilled as the couple returned up the aisle at the conclusion of the ceremony. At the reception in the church parlor Eleanor congratulated Dan and his bride, and then met both sets of parents. Barbara's parents had driven up from Arizona where they had retired in the Phoenix area. The Marinos came from Bigfork to join the festivities. When Eleanor met Dan's parents, Peter and Lidia Marino, shivers went up her spine as she shook Peter's hand, so reminded was she of Landi. The same dark complexion and black hair. She felt more drawn to Dante than ever, and now to his family as well.

At the conclusion of the reception, Dan and is bride left for a three day honeymoon in Yellowstone Park. Eleanor's wedding gift was a three-night stay at the Lake Hotel in the Park.

As Eleanor returned to the Northern, it was with bittersweet joy that she thought about Dan and Barbara at the Lake Hotel. *I am so happy for them, but I wish it could have been Landi and me.*

In the summertime, Eleanor enjoyed walking to work. One morning in July, a month or so after Dan's wedding, she discovered that a small house on her block of Lewis was for rent. She immediately thought of the young Marinos. When she got to work she mentioned this to Dan.

"I might be interested. I'll check it out after work."

"Rentals are snatched up really quickly. I think I'd inquire right away. In fact, why don't you run over and see it. I can take the desk while you do that."

"You sure?"

"Yes. Here's the address." Eleanor handed him a slip of paper with the address.

"O.K. I'll call Barbara and see if she can meet me there."

In less than an hour, Dan returned very excited about the house.

"We both really like the house and we signed up for it right away. We can move in on Saturday."

"Great! That's what I mean about rentals getting snatched the minute they are on the market."

Through the late summer and fall, on Sundays after church Eleanor was frequently invited to picnic in Pioneer Park with friends she had developed at church. Sometimes this included Dan and Barbara. She found other amenities in Billings appealing, especially as winter came and she no longer had yard and gardening activities. She purchased a season ticket to the Billings Symphony and made good use of the Parmly Billings Library.

The next May, Dan brought Barbara home from Deaconess Hospital with their first baby, whom they proudly named Angelina after Dan's mother's middle name, and Gail after Barbara's mother's name. She would come to be called Angie as she became the center of Dan and Barbara's life as a family.

In the week following, Eleanor was among the first to make a visit to see Angelina. The small stuffed puppy she brought would be the first of many gifts she would bring to Angie over the years. When Angie would be a bit older Eleanor would be a willing baby-sitter as well.

On a Sunday morning in August, Angelina's grandparents stood with Dan and Barbara holding Angie before the baptismal font in front of the congregation at First Congregational Church. Eleanor also stood with the family as the baby's godmother. After the church service the family group, including Eleanor, went to the Northern for the baptismal dinner in a private dining room. In a curious way, Eleanor felt bonded to Angelina, almost as if in some mysterious way she represented Landi, whom she had lost so long ago.

That evening in the quiet loneliness of her living room Eleanor sat in her favorite chair for reading. Instead of reading, she re-lived the day she had spent with Angelina and her extended family. During dinner she had sat next to Dan's father. She asked him about his roots in Italy.

"Where did you and your wife come from before moving to the Flathead?"

"We came to the US from Italy, from the town of Castellmmare di Stabia. We were about twenty miles southeast of Naples, right on the bay. It had a very interesting story. Castellmmare di Stabia lies next to the ancient Roman city of Stabiae, which was destroyed by the Vesuvio eruption in AD 79. The castle the city takes its name from, was erected in around the 9th century on a hill commanding the southern side of the Gulf of Naples. As young people, my wife and I worked in the olive groves, but we could see that we wouldn't get very far working for others. So we had opportunity to come to this country and found out about the cherry orchards in western Montana. A cherry producer by the name of Paul Archer hired us to work for him. A few years later he sold us one of his orchards. Now we have our own orchard—*Marino Cherries.*"

When Eleanor heard Castellammare di Stabia, a nameless recognition stabbed her memory. "Why should the name of your town in Italy sound familiar?"

"Perhaps it is because a famous Chicago family came from my home town!"

"Who was that?"

"The Capones! Al Capone's parents came from there. His father had been a barber there."

When Eleanor heard this she was taken aback. "I see. Did you happen to know anybody back home by the name of Ferrini?"

"No, not right off the bat. . . ." He thought some more. "Do you have a first name?"

"Landino FERRINI. . . He would have been about your age."

"Sounds a little familiar. Could have been somebody I knew at school when I was little. Somebody you know?"

"I used to. But he's dead."

"Oh."

At least I think he is

As she thought about that conversation she had a wistful feeling and couldn't get the idea out of her head that little Angelina and Landino came from the same roots. *No wonder I keep seeing him in her little eyes.*

CHAPTER 28

When Landi had returned to Italy he located Loreto as well as his cousin, Maria. This gave Landi a sense of having returned home as well as opportunity to establish himself in his former surroundings. His cousin, Maria and her husband, were especially hospitable and included Landi in their own social circle of friends, which coincidentally included Loreto and Armando. These relationship made Landi feel very much at home in Italy and his experience in the U.S. began to fade.

After Maria's husband, Eduardo, was killed Maria and Landi worked out a partnership in Maria's olive grove business. Landi's participation was to help finance it, and while his full time work would be in the hotel, he worked in the grove during his off hours from his hotel work. In addition to bringing in a little more income to Landi, the fringe benefit to him was a chance to learn the business of keeping a grove of fruit-producing trees.

Sensing that Maria needed more than his hands-on help in the grove, he began the custom of having her for Sunday dinner at his house after she returned from mass. Earlier he had not shared much of his U.S. experience with the Rossi's. Now, after Casey's assurance of safety after Big Al's death, he told Maria a bit about his Chicago days and his years in Montana. Maria had found all this quite fascinating. She was a person who displayed real empathy with others. Landi found himself sharing more and more of his own feelings with his cousin—especially when it came to his memories of Eleanor and his grief over losing her.

"That must be awful for you when you think about that hotel fire, Landi!"

"It is. I try to put it out of my mind, but it comes back."

"I know what you mean. It is the same for me when I think of Eduardo's truck accident."

"Oh, I'm sorry, Maria. Here I have been burdening you with my grief and you have your own to handle."

"That's all right. I have had Father at my church to talk to, but I don't think you have had anyone like that."

"No, you're right. I haven't." This exchange prompted him to tell her about his dream of the fires and of Ellie's "message" to him---*I'm alive, Landi. Come to me.* "Maria, those words haunt me. I don't know whether to believe them, let alone to know what to do about them."

Both were quiet for an extended moment. Then Maria spoke. "Oh, Landi, I'm sure I wouldn't know what to do either." She thought some more. "But, you know, I think I wouldn't be satisfied until I went to the last place I'd been with her. . . and see what happens . . if anything."

"That's sort of what I was afraid to think, for my mind told me that was nonsense."

"That may be, but I don't think so. There are such things as pilgrimages when people go somewhere special to heal their souls."

"I don't know about that. Do you know of such a pilgrimage?"

"Yes, Father told me about The way of St. James, a pilgrimage. A walking path to the Cathedral of Santiago de Compostela in Galicia, Spain, where tradition has it that the remains of the apostle Saint James are buried.. . . but there are lots of other pilgrimages to one holy place or another."

"What is supposed to happen if you walk that route. . . or to some other place?"

"I think it is sort of up to you—whatever you hope and pray for."

"I don't know. Sounds spooky to me."

Their dinner conversation turned to other things at this point, but the pilgrimage idea would come back to Landi later on. Sometime during their dinner, Olivia had jumped up on Maria's lap, and had gone to sleep. When Landi had objected, Maria assured him that she enjoyed having Liv to hold and to pet. Over the next weeks this friendship between Olivia and Maria persisted.

Landi continued to muse over the possibility to returning to the U.S., at least for a visit, but more and more he thought in terms of moving back to the States. He did not want to settle in Chicago, but wanted to see it again. Missoula itself did not appeal to him, but perhaps somewhere else in Montana would be a good place to settle–if he could find work. But it would take more money than he had. And then there was Olivia?

In some ways the high point of his week had become the Sunday dinner with Maria. To one such dinner in early November, Maria brought some important news with an important question. Landi wasn't quite ready to serve the meal he had prepared, so he joined Maria in his living room. When she was seated, Olivia hopped up on her lap. Without any preliminary small talk she began. "Landi, my neighbor, the one with a grove adjoining ours has asked me if I would be willing to sell our grove to him!"

"Wow! I assume that you don't want to sell."

"That's what I felt at first, but now I am inclined to favor selling. That is if you would agree?"

"Would you be able to make it without the income from the olive profits? What is he offering?"

She gave him the figure he offered and she added. "I think I can make it by investing my half and doing some part-time work around town. And, frankly, I am tired of the work involved in the grove, even with you doing as much as you are."

After making some calculations, Landi shared his thinking with his cousin and business partner. "Maria, this could be the financial break I have been wishing for to help me to return to the U.S. How much time do we have before answering your neighbor?"

"I told him that I needed to discuss this with you and see my banker. He gave us two weeks."

The following Sunday, Maria and Landi finalized their determination to sell their olive grove.

"Do you know yet what you will do?" Landi asked his cousin as Olivia took her accustomed nap on her lap.

"Not yet. How about you?"

"I would really like to go to America–at least for a while. . . if I can work it out."

"What's keeping you? You'll have the money from the sale."

"Olivia!"

"I'd love to take her and I get the impression she would like to live with me all the time, not just on Sunday afternoons. . . . better than with you." Maria said with a smirk.

Landi was deep in thought, and then came up with an idea. "And, you know, I am sure you could take my place at the desk of the hotel. Would you like that?"

"That would be wonderful, Landi."

"I'll talk to the owner in the morning."

That night Landi slept more soundly than usual. When he awakened he could only vaguely remember his dream. But in it he saw a walking trail leading ahead of him. Instead of any clear image, he experienced a deeply joyful feeling which he could not explain. However, in the distance he seemed to hear the call. . . *come to me.*

In his dream he tried to answer but he was not sure who had called to him. *But who are you?*

Oh, Landi. . .don't you know me anymore? came a plaintive cry.

Ellie! Is it you, Ellie?

Come to me. . .

PART IV

Pilgrimage

CHAPTER 29

Landino Ferrini sat back in his coach seat aboard the Yankee Clipper on a Pan Am flight leaving London's Heathrow Airport with New York City as his destination. He closed his eyes and imagined the walking path he'd seen in his dreams. He heard again the call *Come to me.* His answer was to begin his personal pilgrimage. He whispered, *I'm on my way–my journey to you, Ellie.* He did not know where the trail would lead him. The purpose of a pilgrimage was the healing of one's soul, Maria had told him. But each pilgrim was to define what his or her particular journey's goal and termination would be. However, this was a decision Landi was as yet unwilling to make. *What will I find at trail's end? I know what I wish l could find. . . but. She died in the fire in the Acme. Is my journey to end in death? So that I may join her? Oh God,* he begged, *Isn't there some other answer. . . but how could there be?*

As his flight continued high above the Atlantic in and out of clouds, Landi felt separated from reality. In his euphoria, he and Ellie were walking hand in hand along the shore of a placid body of water stretching endlessly into the horizon. It was as if time had ceased to measure their existence. The former days of their journeys were gone. There seemed only to be a future into which they were already stepping. But where was that future to be?

Reality began to intrude as Landi felt a slight slowing of the aircraft and the beginning of its decent to earth again. Impatient to be on solid ground, his descent seemed to last forever, until finally he was below the clouds and the land could be seen slanting up toward the aircraft. He would soon be making his journey according to his plan.

The aircraft touched down and began its taxi to the gate. Landi deplaned. After retrieving his luggage, he found a small, very crowded restaurant in the terminal. He entered and located an empty seat along a table with individual customers. As he was being served the person on the other side of the table finished his meal, when he got up and left, a woman quickly took his seat. When Landi saw her after she sat down, a shivery wave went down his spine. *Eleanor!* He thought. Then when she turned her head and began reading the menu. *No, I don't think so. Besides it can't be. Or could it?* Landi felt something like a cold sweat as he slowly recovered from this mysterious shock. A harried waitress brought him his ham sandwich and coffee. *My mind is playing tricks on me. Or is that some kind of a sign?* He couldn't keep from looking at the woman. Once or twice she looked at him with no visible sign of recognition.

He finished his meal and got up and left the restaurant. He engaged a cab to take him to the New York Central terminal. As he rode along the city streets, he concluded that the vision of Eleanor must have been due to the mental confusion which an overseas time lapse sometimes induces.

From New York City, Landi took the New York Central train to Chicago. *It seems to me that my pilgrimage ought to take me to Chicago. That's where my life began to take all sorts of turns.* He stepped down from his coach and walked into Union Station to begin his tour of Chicago. Taking a taxi to the Stevens Hotel on Michigan Boulevard, he booked a room on the seventh floor facing Lake Michigan.

His earlier experience in Chicago had been in the underworld of organized crime. The notable amenities and places to see in the city had been out of reach for him. He had been invisible. So also the city itself. But now he was free to visit the city as a tourist "above ground" so to speak. The only vestige of his past was seen in the way he registered as Harland Ferris in order to hide his past life of Landino Ferrini.

He took great delight in taking many of his meals in the hotel dining room, always alone, of course. He spent the better part of a week "doing the town." He visited the Field Museum of Natural History, and the Adler Planetarium not too far from his hotel. At the Art Institute on Michigan Boulevard he especially enjoyed seeing many of the originals done by Italian artists. He went on a city bus down to Jackson Park and spent a day in the Museum of Science and Industry.

On Sunday morning he took a bus north to Fourth Presbyterian Church on Michigan and Delaware. The entire service of worship moved him deeply. He had never heard such a majestic organ, as it was played by the church organist, Barret Spaeth. He was inspired by the sermon entitled, NOT KNOWING WHITHER HE WENT, delivered by Dr. Harrison Ray Anderson, Sr. The text which summarized his message, and which spoke volumes to Landi, was:

By faith Abraham, when he was called to go out into a place which he should receive for an inheritance, obeyed; and he went out, not knowing whither he went. (Hebrews 11:8)

The gist of the sermon was that Abraham had been an obscure tribal chieftain about three thousand years ago who heard God's call to him, directing him to go to an unknown destination. There he would receive God's inheritance to become the first leader of God's special people. It was Abraham's faith by which he followed God's command without a clue as to where he was going. The point which was made in the sermon was that God calls each of us to go on a pilgrimage of faith, not knowing where this pathway would lead. But if we are faithful, we will receive an inheritance from God.

He found a nearby restaurant where he ordered a Sunday dinner. During dinner he pondered his return to Chicago and decided to try and find the spots which had turned him away from the Capone involvement and where Eleanor had been tainted by it as well. He remembered enough of the Chicago transportation system to be able to make his way up Milwaukee Avenue to the block where he had been involved in the drive-by shooting. He was mentally sickened once again as he re-lived that tragic block.

From what Ellie had told him, he could pretty well locate the sandwich shop where she had worked and where the mob had tried to ensnare her. He made his way back to his downtown location by way of Clark Street, where curiosity led him to find the building in the 2900 block behind which the Valentines Day massacre had been carried out. Again he was sickened by the thought of so vicious an attack.

After this gangland tour, Landi was relieved to return to his hotel room. This had been a stark reminder of the ugly beginning of his American experience, and of Eleanor's introduction to what she had mistakenly hoped would be the delights of the big city. For his final evening in Chicago, he spent most of the time sitting in a chair which gave him a view of the lake. It had been a clear day on which he could gaze on the rippling waves which disappeared in the horizon. The other shore could not be seen. He had a lot to think about as dusk began to darken the glistening waves on the lake. He thought once again of his euphoric daydream over the Atlantic and of the mysterious, almost recognizable, face in the restaurant.. He reviewed the sermon in his mind. At this point he certainly did not know "whither" he was going, but to follow his earlier trek to Montana and well away from Chicago. Where possibly he would "receive an inheritance."

Monday morning found Landi seated in the crowded waiting room in Union Station. He was as yet unsure of his destination in Montana. That question was settled when an older man dressed western with a cowboy hat and boots sat down next to him. He struck up a conversation with Landi.

"Where you headed?"

"Montana, but I don't exactly have it figured where I'll go once I'm there."

"Oh? Where you from?"

"I've come from Italy, but I used to live in Montana, up around Missoula. How about you?"

"I live in Lavina. On a ranch. I have been in Chicago where I dropped off a carload of cattle at the Union Stockyards. Now I head back home. First to Billings where I have my truck at the stockyards. Then I'll drive on home to Lavina."

"Billings?"

"The wife and I like Billings. We get down there to shop every so often. It's only around fifty miles from home. And when we need doctoring we go to the Deaconess Hospital there. Lots of good doctors. . . Billings is quite a city. A medical center for that part of the west and it's got a couple of colleges. The wife, she got a teaching degree at Eastern there. She teaches fourth grade in the Lavina school. But my boy, he's going to the ag school in Bozeman. Someday he'll take over the ranch. Already he's learned stuff that sort of makes me feel old fashioned around the place. But that's all right. . . progress, I guess. When he takes over, he'll be the third generation on the land."

The more he spoke about Billings the more interested Landi became. The result was that Landi purchased a ticket to Billings and the two rode together. It was a long overnight train trip in which both men had taken coach seats. True to the unwritten "law of the old west" they did not exchange their names but became friends at least temporarily.

At one point the older man asked, "Tell me a little bit more about your experience in Montana and what you hope for now."

"Well, I want to see some of the places I lived in before. . . around Missoula where I did

some commercial hauling. I'll need to find work."

"Hauling?"

"Or work in the orchards up on the Flathead. I learned the orchard business when I had part ownership of an olive grove in Italy. . . if I can find something up there in an orchard . . . ."

After thinking about what the younger man had said. "You know— the wife has a brother who has an orchard south of Bigfork. Tell you what. . . His name is Archer. I'll give you directions to his orchard and he might have work." He reached in his pocket for a pencil and a piece of paper and wrote the directions for Landi.

"That would be great ."

At that point the lights in the coach were dimmed and pillows were passed out. The two men slept as best as they could while the train rolled through Minnesota and North Dakota.

When they came near Billings Landi asked his new acquaintance, "Do you know of any good hotels in Billings where I might stay for a few days before I figure out what's next?"

"By far the best is the Northern Hotel just a few blocks west of the depot. Second best, I'd say, is the Custer also just west."

After the train pulled into the station, the two men stepped onto the platform and bid each other goodbye. After retrieving his checked luggage, Landi hired a cab and went to the Northern. He asked the cab driver to wait while he checked to see if there was a room available. He walked into the impressive lobby and up to the desk.

"Do you have a room for two or three nights?"

"Let me check, sir." After looking, he replied. "We might have. Depends on one party who has not yet shown. Let me check with the manager."

Landi watched as the desk clerk walked over through a glass office door with the brass plate indicating manager. As he went in, Landi could see the back of a woman at her desk. The clerk soon returned.

"I'm sorry, I am told that the party is on the way. But I could call the Custer for you, if you want."

"Please do." Again as he waited, he observed the back of the woman manager in her office. Something seemed to pull on his mind, but he did not know what that was all about.

"They have a room available and will hold it for ten minutes until you can go over there."

Landi re-entered his cab and asked to be taken to the Custer. He checked in as Harland Ferris, and the bellman took his suitcases which the cabby had deposited in the lobby. The bellman ushered Landi into his room on the third floor. After tipping him, Landi sat down to ponder what was next in his journey. He counted the funds he had for the rest of his journey.

When Landi had left Naples he deposited the bulk of his half of the sale from the grove. But he took an ample supply of lira with him which he converted into American Express Travelers Checks when he had arrived in New York City.

A plan began to take shape for the next leg of his pilgrimage in Montana, the first step of which would take place the next morning when he walked down First Avenue North to Archie Cochrane's Ford dealership. He checked out the line up of used pick ups on the lot. He found a 1939 Ford pickup which suited him, and which he could afford— after a bit of dickering with the salesman.

He drove off the lot into the next phase of his journey. His pilgrimage pattern of going back to former haunts was beginning to take shape and so now he determined to re-trace his earlier experience in Montana, beginning with a re-visit to Illinois City—what was left of his first home in Montana.

He passed over the continental divide on Homestake Pass and into Butte. He found a room at the Legate to which he had once delivered some furniture. The next morning Landi headed west toward Illinois City. When the tall stack came into view he decided to drive into Anaconda. He slowly drove by the Montana Hotel where his last night in Montana had been spent. When he passed the place where he had been abducted by the Mob, shivers went through his body. He remembered vividly that night. He had thought *surely they will take me away somewhere, kill me and dump my body in a hidden location. Then they will disappear. They will return to report their work to Big Al.* Landi had been terrified.

Worst of all, he could not let Ellie know what was happening. *I'll never see her again.*

He drove around to the rear of the Hotel and saw the spot where he had parked his truck, now occupied by a passenger car, most likely belonging to one of the guests. He sped away and onto the highway, heading toward Illinois City. Once agin needing to escape the clenching fists of the Mob.

CHAPTER 30

The now-abandoned mining town of Illinois City had been far up a particular drainage in the mountains of western Montana, to which there once had been a railroad spur line of the Northern Pacific Railroad winding up to a gold mine from which the ore was hauled down to the mill where the gold was extracted. This spur line also carried passenger trains. Landi had been one of its passenger when he first arrived, seemingly so long ago. Landi discovered that the tracks had been torn up many years ago, leaving only a winding set of rocky wagon ruts along which to reach the ghost town. In its heyday 3,000 people had lived in the town in the '80s. and '90's. Fewer by the time Landi had lived there.

It was at almost dusk when he came up against a slight rise leading to a particularly dense barrier of foliage. At this point there was an ancient wooden sign with its painted message faintly visible-- "Trail's End." He could see that this would be as far as he could drive his vehicle. He could see, however, the nearly invisible impressions on the ground where once there had been rails leading beyond the barrier. And so he made his way through the dense growth and mounted the rise until he could look far ahead and below. There the ghost of Illinois City hovered beneath his vantage point at the terminus of the rail markings.

After so many years since leaving Illinois City, seeing the town again before his eyes was an emotional experience for Landi. He sat down on a protruding rock and simply looked over this town. What was left of the structures were clustered along what appeared to be four intersecting streets. The overall scene was one of ancient brown weathered wood blending into the dark hues of the dusty soil spackled with dried weeds. In varying stages of decay, some of the buildings were still remarkably intact and recognizable. A few of these remnants were two-storied. The rest were one story and squat. Many of the roofs remained. Now under the rising moon some of the window openings throughout the town reflected splashes of silver indicating that some of the glass panes remained. He remembered with an eerie feeling that this town, once busy and populated with people of all ages, had suddenly died; after the tragic events which had happened to cause everyone in town to leave—all of them over a relatively short period of time. Like the mysterious disappearance of the dinosaurs. *I was one of these forced to abandon the town.*

It had gotten late, too late. So Landi set out to return down the winding trail as quickly as he could with only the waning light of dusk and his dimmed memory to guide him. In time he was relieved to reach his Ford pickup, which he had parked as far up the hill as he could. As he began his drive to a hotel for the night, he knew this would not be his last trip up to Illinois City. In fact, as he observed collapsed structures amid the encroaching grass and weeds, he felt a certain urgency to reclaim his life in Illinois City. He would try to identify particular houses in which the people in this town had lived, and the places where they had labored. *And where Ellie and I lived and fell in love.*

Landi made his way to Bearmouth Lodge, which was still in operation. He booked a room for the night. He went to bed with so many thoughts of the days he had spent with Ellie. He returned to Illinois City the next morning early enough in the day to walk the vacant streets of this once-bustling town.

When he entered the town, he was overwhelmed with the empty stillness. The only sounds were those of a gentle breeze and the distant calling of wild birds. He tried to identify from memory as best as he could most of the dwellings and commercial buildings.

While some of the houses had been built with rough hewn logs, most of the structures appeared to him to be stud and frame construction built around the turn of the century. One building along the continuation of the road into town appeared to have been the three-storied hotel. Next to the hotel was a two-floored building which had been a lodge hall. Next to this lodge hall was a fair sized building with glass display windows, mostly cracked or broken. Over its front door was a weathered sign proclaiming *"MERCANTILE."* Lined up near these two, as well as across what was probably Main Street, were a few smaller buildings, most likely the other shops of one sort or another. The town had been laid out on a slight rising grade. On the street one block above Main street were the two churches, one on each end of town. The smaller of two churches was St. Ignatius Catholic Church, and the larger one on the other end of town was. Asbury Methodist. A lane along the upper edge of the town had two imposing houses somewhat larger than the ones below them. One was a plain square house two stories high, its second floor apparently of equal size to the first floor. It had a simple outside stair steps leading to a small porch and a front door over which was an overhanging roof. This house was where the Moretti family had lived. Behind it was the flattened debris of the carriage house. *This was my home!*

The house next door had been where Eleanor lived and worked, with its two peaked roof lines at right angles and a small wraparound porch, had been a Sears Roebuck Catalogue home. It was a six room house with three bedrooms on the second floor. It had been known as *The Mayor's Mansion*. The owner of the mines lived there and for many years he had been the unofficial Mayor of Illinois City. *That's where Ellie lived and worked.*

After a couple hours, Landi left Illinois City. It had been a bittersweet experience for him, so good to remember their lives here, yet so saddened to know that not only had the town died, but Ellie was gone from his life as well. He reluctantly turned toward the almost obscure trail leading him away from Illinois City, letting it return to the flora and fauna of the natural environment which had already been gradually absorbing this quaint village of Landi's former days. *Where Ellie and I met and fell in love.*

For Landi, seeing the sagging remains of the town was like seeing a drama on a stage with a live cast on it. . . and then having the curtain drawn. . . and now reopened to find the set without any live actors upon the Illinois City stage .

On that lifeless stage on which the drama of Illinois City had been enacted, Landi saw now the buildings in which the leading actors had made their entrances and their exits. He thought of their final exits off stage disappearing into the darkness behind the curtain forever. He cast a final glance at what was left of the Mayor's Mansion, and of the Carriage House behind Moretti's house.

As Landi again left Illinois City, this time forever, he yearned to go back in time and to be with Ellie again.

The debris-strewn empty stage which once had been lively Illinois City depressed Landi deeply. He almost wished he hadn't returned. The scene of destruction seemed to verify his sad feeling of his loss of Ellie

As Landi returned to his pickup and passed by the wooden sign along the way out which had announced Trail's End, he thought about what came after the end of Illinois City for him and for Ellie.

That evening Landi drove into Missoula and was mysteriously drawn to the site of the Acme Hotel where Eleanor had worked as a chambermaid. He braced himself to see charred ruins from the fire which must have consumed Ellie. He prepared himself for the acrid smell of charred wood and of death. To his amazement he found not the charred ruins but a re-built hotel.

At a sudden urging he stopped and checked in for the night. Later, when he climbed between the fresh smelling laundered sheets he thought to himself in anguish. *If only Ellie could be returned to me.*

He dreamed that night a vague and diffuse dream, but somehow when he awakened he knew that he had been near Ellie. He thought he heard her calling again *Landi, come to me.* Later as he thought about his dream he wondered, *Could Ellie–in some mysterious way–be the goal of my pilgrimage? By faith—not knowing where I am going—like Abraham to the promised land.*

The next morning as he looked around the small lounge near the desk he found a plaque hanging on the wall commemorating the tragedy of the fire. He braced himself when he read the list of hotel staff who had lost their lives in the fire, expecting to read Eleanor's name. But she was not listed. *I wonder why. . . could it be that she was not among the lost? Otherwise why was she not listed?* he pondered as he left the Acme to find a spot for breakfast.

While he ate, his attention turned to matters more practical and pressing. He needed to find work if he was to remain in this part of Montana. His only lead was the slip of paper his rancher friend from the train had given him. The man's brother-in-law, Paul Archer, who has an orchard near Bigfork--- this is where he would go to seek work.

After breakfast in Missoula, he stopped for a fill up on gas in Polson. While there, he asked about the best way to get to Bigfork and the area in which there were orchards.

The attendant gave him directions. "Just go up the east shore which you pick up on the south end of town. Drive north and you eventually will come to orchards, and then you'll soon go through Woods Bay and then you'll just about be at Bigfork."

Landi thanked the service station clerk and drove out of Polson on his way-- *to work, I hope.* Before leaving Main Street he saw that preparations were underway for some sort of fair, which he soon learned was the annual cherry festival. He turned onto highway 35 just south of town and headed toward Bigfork and the orchards. At Woods Bay he stopped in at a small cafe for coffee at the counter. He asked a man next to him. "You wouldn't happen to know a Paul Archer, would you?"

"Why sure, everybody knows Archer. He's a big operator around here."

"Where can I find him?"

"Go back toward Polson and you'll see his sign *ARCHER ORCHARDS* a few miles south of here."

When Landi came to the sign he saw also a temporary notice--*Help Wanted.* This gave him an automatic "in" when he knocked at the door "I'm Harland Ferris. I saw your sign asking for help."

"Yes, I'm looking for some help to truck my produce to Polson for the festival. tomorrow, and also up to Kalispell next week."

"I can do that. I have a pick-up and I used to haul in a large sized truck out of Missoula. By the way, I met your brother-in-law in the train station in Chicago and rode with him to Billings. He told me about your place here."

"Yeah, he's on that train at least once a year with a load of cattle. Cherries are a lot easier to market than cows, but he does well. Anyway, be here tomorrow-Friday-at 6:30 and you have a job, at least temporarily."

As it turned out he made two trips to Polson to the Archer booth, and was back in Bigfork by early afternoon checking into a motel.

This lead could not have turned out better. Archer needed a man with a pickup to help during the time of the cherry festival in Polson. Landi was put to work immediately. He found a room to rent in Bigfork.

Archer had also put Landi in touch with his neighbor, Peter Marino. "I believe Pete also needs help in preparation for the festival. . . I'll give him a ring and tell him about you."

Landi drove over to Marino's. "Mr. Archer sent me to see if you need any help."

"As a matter of fact, I do. What's your name?"

"Harland Ferris. . . but originally I was Landino Ferrini."

"Really. You from Italy?"

"Yes, from the Naples region, but I have been here since I was a young man, and in fact, I recently lived there and was part owner of an olive grove."

"Well, we have been neighbors in the old country. I came from Naples. My family came over when I was quite young. So did Luisa's family. . . about the same time."

"That's very interesting, sir."

"You asked about work. I can use you during the festival to haul my cherries to Polson. Then we can see if there might be other work here. OK?"

"Very much so.

Despite the fact that Landi's primary responsibility was to Paul Archer, he was given work for the Marino's as well. Their common roots in Italy gave him a special connection.

CHAPTER 31

In the months following Angelina's birth and baptism, Eleanor's relationship with the Marino family deepened, often baby sitting little Angie and spending some of the holiday meals and celebrations with the family. In July after Angelina's third birthday, Dan dropped into Eleanor's office. "This is not hotel business but I wanted to invite you to over to Polson with us for the annual cherry festival next month. My parents and a lot of their neighbors will be there displaying their produce."

"Sounds like fun. I'd enjoy seeing your folks again Dan, as well as the festival, if the dates work out." They checked the dates on Eleanor's official calendar. "I think that will work."

"Great! You can ride with us."

"Thank you, but as I think about it, I have been wanting to spend a little time in Missoula where I worked as a young woman. I can do that and then meet you up in Polson."

It was decided then that Eleanor would go up on Thursday, and then meet all the Marinos on Friday in time for the festival.

Eleanor had heard that the Acme in Missoula had been re-built after the fire and she was curious to see it. A wave of sad nostalgia made her want to be in Missoula again. When she arrived on Thursday night of the festival weekend, she found that the rebuilding of the Acme had pretty well followed the original design, so she felt somewhat at home as she checked in at the desk.

It was a lonely night in her room as the painful wound of her loss of Landi intensified in this place where earlier in their lives she had been near him.

Friday morning, after a quick breakfast at a nearby café, Eleanor began her drive up to Flathead through the Flathead reservation. She was quite taken with the Mission Range on her right, rising so majestically from the flat expanse of the valley. She drove north passing by the town of St. Ignatius. Towering above the town was the tall steeple of the St. Ignatius mission church dating back to the 1890s.

She drove further north through Ronan. Soon she came to Polson, where she first caught sight of Flathead Lake spread in front of her. Following Dan's directions, she took the East Shore Road and eventually passed through to neat cherry orchards on both sides of the road. She found the Marino Orchard just south of Bigfork. She arrived in time for lunch with the Marino family, after which they all went to Polson for the Cherry Festival on Main Street.

Like a farmers market each producer had a booth from which he or she sold boxes of fresh cherries from their orchard. The booth next to Marino's was occupied by their neighbors further up on the the East Shore, George and Jesse Crane. As second generation keepers of the orchard, they were somewhat younger than Peter and Lydia Marino. When Jesse and Eleanor met there was a sort of instant attraction which made for easy conversation as they became acquainted with each other.

"Did you grow up here on the lake?" Eleanor asked.

"No, I grew up in Missoula. This was George's home. He went to the university. That's where we met."

"When I was quite a bit younger I lived in Missoula for a while."

"You did? Where?"

Eleanor was reluctant to say much. "Yes, I worked in a downtown hotel. The Acme."

"Really! That's the one that burned down."

"Yes, but fortunately for me I had left the Acme a few days before. My original home had been in Iowa. So miraculously, a few days before the fire I left Missoula after I had decided it was time for me to return to my parents's home in Iowa, at least for a visit, if not for a move."

"What made you want to leave Montana?"

Eleanor was hesitant to continue but Jesse seemed to be a very caring questioner. "Well, I was engaged to a young man I had met and we had fallen in love. We were planning to be married but. . . ."

"But?"

"He was a truck driver. . . he had his own business. He was hauling a load to Anaconda when. . . some people he had worked for in Chicago abducted him and later killed him."

"Why?"

"He knew too much. Their business was shady, to say the least."

"Oh."

"Well anyway, I didn't know all of this at the time, only that he never came back to me in Missoula. It was later that I came to realize what had happened."

"I'm so sorry, Eleanor."

"Thank you, Jesse. . . But I have moved on, and now I'm working in a hotel in Billings. I guess hotels for me are kinda like cherries to you!"

"That's how you got to know the Marinos?"

"Yes, through Dan, whom I had hired to work on the desk, which reminds me, I really need to get back to Billings. . . to see what's left of the Northern." She said with a glint in her eye. "I have certainly enjoyed being up here on the Flathead and especially meeting you and Peter."

"It's been our pleasure, Eleanor. I hope you and I can keep in touch, and that you'll be back again."

"I agree, and I'm sure I'll return."

CHAPTER 32

After the festival, Landi was needed by both the Archer and Marino orchards during harvest. Both producers hired him to haul cherries to the gathering place not far from Yellow Bay on the east shore.

When the work slacked off, Landi was invited to the Marinos for an eggplant parmesan dinner. During the meal Luisa asked, "How did you come to be up here on the Flathead?"

"Well, on my trip west I met Paul Archer's brother-in-law, and he mentioned that I might find some work with him. He told me a lot about Billings. So that's where I got off and spent a few days there before continuing my trek to Missoula, where my fiancee' once lived."

"Our son, Dan, lives in Billings. He's assistant manager of the Northern Hotel."

"I tried to get a room there when I first arrived, but they were full. The manager reminded him of a special group coming in, which would need all the available rooms."

"Dan and his manager are good friends."

After the dinner, Landi expressed his appreciation. "Thanks so much for including me in your dinner this evening. It was like being back in Italy again."

"We enjoyed having you."

In time, his jobs with both Archer and Marino would give Landi contact with others along the shore for whom he could do similar hauling. Among his new customers were George and Jesse Crane whose booth at the festival had been next to the Marino booth. Like the Archers and the Marinos, the Cranes treated Landi like a neighbor rather than some nameless trucker or other. Whenever she had a chance to chat with Landi, Jesse Crane would pump Landi about Italy, espeically about the traditional food.

Aa a result of the friendship developing with the Archers and the Marinos, and now the Cranes, Landi came to see himself remaining in this area of Montana—that is, if he could pick up enough work. He remained in the Bigfork area until after harvest, then he sought hauling jobs more widely in the Kalispell and Bigfork areas. He had found a small apartment in Bigfork and felt quite settled. Except for the nagging realization that his pilgrimage perhaps had not come to an end. *What am I looking for? Where am I finally to go? Might I ever find some trace of Ellie? Her name wasn't on the plaque . . . .*

After cherry season work had slowed down for Landi. As the roadside cherry stands were boarded up for another year, Landi had only some clean up work to do at Marinos, and that would soon end. To celebrate the conclusion of a good year, Peter and Luisa invited Landi for a Sunday dinner, when the Marinos returned home from mass Landi came to the house.

After a fried chicken dinner followed, of course, with cherry pie, Peter and Landi relaxed in the living room. Peter asked, "What do you plan to do now that your work is over?"

"I'm not sure. I may go back to Anaconda and Butte where I did some hauling before. It looks like nothing much is left up here on the Flathead."

"I'm sorry. Not until next spring." He thought about Landi's situation. "Will you let your apartment go, if you go down to Butte?"

"That's probably what I should do, but I won't move my stuff. I guess I'll find a storage facility until I find something permanent."

"You can store it here in one of our buildings on the place."

"That's good of you to offer. I just may take you up on it."

Luisa joined the men and the conversation turned to other matters. At one point Luisa asked Peter, "Did you know that the Cranes went on a pilgrimage to the Basilica of the Immaculate Conception in Washington?"

"No. How was it for them?"

"She was quite moved by the whole experience. She said it helped her clear up a lot of things she had been worried about."

"I'm surprised. They aren't Catholic."

"I know. They are Methodist. But I believe a lot of people go on pilgrimages, no matter what, if any, faith they might profess."

Peter then reminisced, "I remember when I was a boy in Italy, people used to go on a pilgrimage along the Via Francigena. Did you know about that Luisa?"

"The Sisters used to talk about it. There were a lot of walking trails from France into Italy, I think. Did you ever hear about that, Landi? Some of them were on old Roman roads."

"Not really, only that I was told that people sometimes went on pilgrimages to help them with their lives."

Soon it was time for Landi to leave and he thanked them for the meal and the fellowship of the afternoon.

That night in his apartment he thought about the conversation with the Marinos. *I can't believe how often this idea of pilgrimages has come up. I wonder if God is trying to tell me something? Maybe my pilgrimage has only begun. First to Illinois City where Ellie and I met and fell in love. Then to Missoula where we parted. . . forever? I thought so but. . .? Where else could the trail lead?*

As Landi thought about some of the last conversations he and Eleanor had with each other, he remembered that she had said that she wished she could go back to Iowa sometime to her childhood home. He had said that he would like to return to Italy someday. He had returned to his roots. *I wonder if she did.*

He went to bed wondering if she had ever returned to her home and parents in Iowa. During the night, from time to time he experienced one of those diffuse dreams in which one cannot really tell what is going on. In his dream a picture of Ellie's house in Iowa, as she had described it, seemed to reappear. At first it was in the distance seeming to be beyond him on a walking trail. At another time it seemed closer to him. But Ellie would never appear.

The next morning, the vision of Ellie's house down a tree-lined walking trail persisted in Landi's mind. *My pilgrimage,* he thought. What had begun as a pilgrimage to re-visit the places where he and Ellie had been together now was turning into a pilgrimage to find Eleanor. *I have found out that she hadn't been burned to death in the Acme fire, so the question I must answer is where she is now.*

A plan for the next phase of his pilgrimage began to take shape. He felt an urgency to get on the trail again. He bought some canvas at a hardware store in Kalispell with which he covered the box of his pickup. He already had a bed roll and he picked up other items at the store in order to equip his vehicle for overnight camping.

While in the hardware store, Landi ran into George and Jesse Crane. "What are you up to?" George asked.

"I'm getting myself equipped for overnight camping in my pickup."

"Oh?" Jesse responded.

"Yeah I'm heading back to Iowa. . .some folks I want to see."

"Why don't you have lunch with us here in town before you go," Jesse suggested.

"Sounds good."

While waiting for their sandwiches in a nearby café, Landi asked Jesse and George to tell him about their experience on the pilgrimage in D.C. Jesse was quite animated as she described the pilgrimage

"This sort of thing is new to me but I am intrigued. I guess it is because I have some unresolved questions and I've been told that pilgrimages help people in their search for answers."

"That was our experience," George agreed.

Jesse was quiet for a moment and then added, "We were told that you don't have to go to some exotic place, but that wherever you are you can pursue your quest, whatever it is."

"Well, thanks for sharing with me."

Their lunches arrived and their conversation turned to lighter things until they were finished and took their separate ways.

He closed out his apartment and headed south to Missoula. He dropped in on the Marinos to tell them goodbye for a while. "I will plan to be back in the spring and if you need my help at that time I'll be glad to have the work."

"You can count on it," Peter assured him. "Where will you spend the winter?" he asked.

"I'm not sure. I want to make some contacts in Missoula and I may go east."

"Well, be sure and see us when you return,"

With that, Landi went on his way toward Missoula.

He found a spot to camp along the Blackfoot River just east of Bonner. The next morning he wasted no time driving into Missoula and to the boarding house in which Eleanor had lived while working at the Acme. By this time it was under a dilfferent ownership, but he stepped up to the door and asked about Eleanor just the same.

"I'm afraid that was too long ago for me to know anything about her," the new owner replied.

"Are there any old timers around who might have known her?"

"No, but I do remember getting a Christmas card from one of the girls. She's now a teacher somewhere in Gallatin County."

"Can you find the card?"

"Oh no. That's long gone, but I do remember her last name. . . Let's see. . . I think it was Visser. That's a Dutch name, I think."

"Well, thanks for your help."

As he drove away, Landi tried to remember if he had heard of anyone with that name. It was vaguely familiar at first---and then he thought of Ellie's room mate, Dorothy. *I think her name was Dorothy Visser. . .and I believe she had come from Amsterdam, Montana. . . That's a Dutch town.* He then got out his Montana road map and found Amsterdam and discovered that it's in Gallatin County. *If anyone will know anything about Ellie, it would be Dorothy. I need to find Dorothy.*

After a quick hamburger at a local café, Landi hit the trail again, driving east toward Amsterdam where he hoped to find Dorothy Visser. When darkness began to descend, Landi located a campground near Three Forks at the Missouri Headwaters Park.

The next morning, Landi ate breakfast in a cafe in Manhattan. He asked the waitress."How do I get to Amsterdam?"

"Just take highway 288 south from here. It's only about ten miles and you"ll be there. You'll see a sign for Amsterdam, but there is not much there. Just go a little further and you'll be in what's called Church Hill. It's where the people live who aren't still out on the farms nearby."

Landi paid for his breakfast, got into his pickup and followed the directions to Amsterdam and he drove into Church Hill. He saw a very large church which looked to him rather European. Its sign read "First Christian Reformed Church." There was hardly anything else in the very small town. He stopped when he saw an old man walking with a cane. "Can you tell me where I might find a Dorothy Visser?"

"Well now, there are an awful lot of Vissers around here. Your best bet would be to go into the church and ask them that's working in there."

Landi parked and went in. He found a door with PASTOR on it and he rapped.

"Come in."

"How do you do, sir. I'm looking for a Dorothy Visser. Do you know where I might locate her?"

"Yes. She is one of our teachers in our Christian School just behind the church. If you go there the lady in the office can help you."

"Thank you, Father."

"It's Pastor."

"Sorry, sir."

Landi left the church building and walked back to the school house, where he found the office and repeated his request

"Yes, Dorothy is one of our teachers—fourth grade. But she won't be free until after school. Around 3:15."

"I'll come back then. Would you give her a note with my name on it and that I'll be back at 3:15?"

"Certainly."

"My name is Landino Ferrini."

CHAPTER 33

Miss Visser took her tray and sat down by herself in the lunch room of Manhattan Christian School. She often ate alone. In fact her life was lonely, with only her fourth grade to keep her in constant contact. She missed her earlier days in Missoula when she was getting her degree from the University of Montana. She had fond memories of living in the boarding house with her roommate Eleanor. After Eleanor had left to return to Iowa, Dorothy kept on in a single room. At first the two had corresponded, but as time went on letters were fewer and fewer until she no longer heard from Eleanor. In fact, she had lost track after Eleanor had moved out of the family house in Ft. Madison. *I miss her. . . I wonder whatever happened to her.*

Her reverie was interrupted when a student office volunteer dropped off a note from the officer onto Dorothy's tray. *Probably an announcement of some meeting I'm supposed to go to,* she thought as she unfolded it preparing to read it. The back of her neck tingled and a shiver went up and down her spine when she read:

> *Miss Visser:*
> *A Mr. Landino Ferrini came to the office looking for you.*
> *He will be here at 3:15 after school today to see you*
> *Anna VanCleave, Office Secretary.*

She sat staring at the note, unable to formulate any clear thought. Disturbed by what she saw, one of Dorothy's fellow teachers came over to ask her what was the matter.

"Dorothy! Did someone pass away?"

"No! Just the opposite. . . I mean. . . ."

"What in the world do you mean?"

Dorothy collected her wits enough to make a reasonable explanation. "A man I assumed was dead just came by, stopped at the office and he wants to see me after school. . . . or at least it is someone with the same name."

Just then the bell rang and it was time to get back to their classrooms. "I'll explain later."

As Dorothy returned her lunch tray and walked back to her class room, she could think of no reasonable explanation. During the rest of the school day she had a difficult time concentrating upon the classwork she was conducting. Time dragged on, until finally the school day closing bell rang. On the one hand she was relieved and couldn't wait to see Landino, but she was also nervous about meeting him after all these years of thinking him dead. She had no idea what to expect. The fourth graders filed out, eager to get home. . . except for little Lillian who came up to Miss Visser's desk with a problem with one of her subjects. She frequently remained after school for some extra help, which normally Dorothy was happy to provide. But today it tried the teachers patience to have to remain an extra five minutes.

After the child left, Dorothy hurriedly patted down her hair and straightened her dress before hurrying down the corridor to meet the man she thought had been killed. There he was, standing alone just inside the outer door, dressed in blue jeans and a denim work shirt. She couldn't read his face until it exploded into recognition. "Dorothy!" he shouted, reaching out his arms.

"Landi!" she replied, accepting his hug. "However did you get here? We thought you were dead, killed by the Mob."

"It's a long story. I'm trying to find Eleanor. I thought she'd been burned to death in the Acme fire, and I found out that didn't happen. Or at least I don't think so. Now where is she?"

"There's too many people around. Let's go somewhere to talk."

"Come out to my pickup. It's just up by the church."

When the two were seated in Landi's Ford, Dorothy told what she could of Eleanor's whereabouts. "First off, let me assure you. She was not in the Acme when it burned down. She had already left for Iowa."

"That's a relief, after all these months and years of thinking of her in the fire."

"The last I heard of her, she was in Iowa at her family home. She wrote me when her mother died. Her father had passed away before she got back After that I never heard again. All I can suggest is that you'll find her back in Ft. Madison, Iowa. But I don't know."

"I see. . . But now I know she's alive."

"Now, please tell me what happened to you. Eleanor told me before she left Montana that you had gone to Anaconda on a trucking job but never came back to Missoula. She waited and waited, and then sometime later she found a news item about a killing by the Mob in Chicago. She took this to mean that you had been the victim. So what really happened?"

"A couple of thugs from the Capone gang abducted me in Anaconda and held me captive. They took me back to Big Al. He forced me to work for him again, but I found a way to escape. And I eventually went back home to Italy. It was only after I heard that Capone had been imprisoned by the federal government on tax evasion that I came back to the U.S.. . . then while in Missoula, I went to the rebuilt Acme and discovered from a plaque on the lobby wall the names of the hotel employees who had lost their lives in the fire. Eleanor was not listed as one of the staff killed in the fire. As a result of this realization I have started on a pilgrimage to find Ellie. . . and that's what brings me here, Dorothy."

Dorothy reached over and touched Landi's hand and said. "Oh Landi, I feel for you and I just wish I could be of more help to you."

"Thank you, Dorothy. I'll just have to keep searching . . . You have already given me a great deal of comfort."

"And I know how absolutely happy Eleanor would be if you found her and she discovered you're alive."

They both were quiet for a long time. There was nothing more which could be said. Until Dorothy offered, "Would you like to come to my apartment for supper, before you continue your search?"

"Yes, if it's no trouble?"

"None at all. Besides, I'd like to visit with you more since both of us have missed Eleanor all these years."

Dorothy's apartment was small and cozy, having the effect of making Landi feel very much at home. "I'll be just a moment. I need to take these school clothes off and put on something more relaxing. Do you mind waiting a bit for supper?"

"No, not all. You go right head." Landi watched her disappear into her bedroom and close the door behind her. He had found the tall blond woman attractive in every way. Such a contrast from the olive skinned brunettes he had known in Italy. He had tried dating a few whom he met there, but he could never let go of his love for Ellie. At least he could share memories of Eleanor with Dorothy. He was eager for her to return to him so that they could talk about Ellie. Soon her door opened and she emerged wearing a fresh white tee shirt over tight-fitting jeans.

"Now, I'll get us some supper."

"Can I help?"

"You might set the table. The things are in the cupboard over there."

"I'll do it." Landi began his task while Dorothy prepared a simple supper. He had some strange feelings—a mixture of a sense of doing something daring and wrong, but at the same time of an intriguing sense of having entered a new and exciting experience. He could almost imagine that he and Eleanor were here in this cozy home about to join in a romantic dinner together.

When Dorothy had put supper on the table she invited Landi to sit down opposite her. "We'll have our blessing first," she said, as she reached across the table to take Landi's hand. Bowing her head she prayed. "Oh God, thank you for this food and for Landi who has come to find his love. We pray for Eleanor, that she may be well and blessed. Bring these two of your children together again. Bless this food and Landi as he makes his pilgrimage to find Eleanor Helm. In Jesus name. Amen."

Landi was moved almost to tears as his new friend prayed and gave his hand a squeeze before letting go. "Thank you, Dorothy."

The two ate the simple supper Dorothy had hastily prepared.

After the meal, they sat in the tiny living room, Dorothy in an easy chair, Landi on a sofa which could be turned into a bed. Landi began, "Tell me about Eleanor when you and she were room mates in Missoula."

After thinking about the question, Dorothy replied. "She was a quiet person and very accommodating, always making me feel comfortable. She didn't enter into any social life. What little of that I had was in connection with my college life. Somehow she seemed older and more mature than the girls I did things with from the University. The more I got to know her, the more I understood that she had been through a maturing process in her life especially in Chicago."

"Did she tell you much about her time in Chicago?"

"Not really. Just in general terms that she had seen the seamy side of life there. So different from my background here in this little old Amsterdam, Montana. . . I guess that was one reason we enjoyed each other so much. Each of us tended to romanticize the life of the other. She saw in my background something of the life she had left in Iowa. . .and that made her sad. I, a naive farm girl was eager to hear all about the big city life."

"Was she happy?"

"No, Landi, she was not. Your absence from her life and then her cruel conclusion that you had been killed snuffed out any chance for what I would call normal happiness."

"That hurts me to hear that."

"I can see that. First her total separation from her family, for which she felt so guilty, and then losing you so tragically. . . that accounted for our closeness, I think. She reached out to me without consciously knowing that. . . And you know as I think about this now, I believe Eleanor brought out a sort of mothering instinct in me. Not to a debilitating extent, just a bit."

"I'm glad she had you. I wonder about her emotional needs now."

"I believe this is why I encouraged her to return to Iowa and to reconcile with her parents. I have often wondered since then if I should have pushed her so hard to go back. Maybe that's why she quit writing."

"No, Dorothy, I am glad you persuaded her." Then wanting to change the subject of their conversation he asked, "Dorothy, tell me your story since Ellie left Missoula."

"Not too exciting. I got my degree from the University of Montana and got a teaching position here at Manhattan Christian School. I have been here ever since. At first I lived with my parents who were still alive when I started here, but after they passed away I got myself this apartment."

"And. . . . ?"

"And what about marriage? You are asking? But afraid to?"

"Well, yes."

"I was single for quite a while but a few years ago I met a widower who farmed out west of town. But right now Gerald is in the Navy. . . due to be discharged in a month. Then, if things are still the way I hope, we'll marry and I'll become a farmer's wife."

"Congratulations. Will you miss teaching?"

"At first, I suppose, but ever since I was a little girl I wanted to be a farm wife."

"I think that sounds great. . . but now, it's getting late. I should be shoving off. This has been a very good evening for me."

"What is the next segment of your pilgrimage as you refer to it?"

"Thanks to what you have told me, I can now say for sure that the next leg of my journey is Iowa—to look for Ellie in Iowa, if my old pickup will make it. Which reminds me. Can you give me her old address which you used?"

"Yes. It is 1320 Avenue I, Ft. Madison, Iowa." Dorothy thought about Landi's trip. "It's getting dark. Won't you stay here overnight. It's Friday night and no school tomorrow. I can fix you a good breakfast before you get away."

"It's that or else I need to find a spot to roll out my bed roll for the night. I'll take you up on it—thank you so much. . . you sure that's ok. . . with the neighbors, I mean!"

"Sure. You and I trust each other and that's all that counts, isn't it?"

"I guess you are right."

With that, she opened up the day bed couch and fixed it up for Landi.

The next morning after a scrumptious breakfast of bacon, eggs, and fried potatoes—all locally grown, Landi departed Amsterdam for his drive to Billings for the night. Before leaving they promised each other to keep in touch. "Please, Landi, if—I mean *when*- you find Ellie let me know. I want to see her almost as much as you do."

CHAPTER 34

It was a beautiful Saturday afternoon when Eleanor Helm, manager, stepped out of the Northern Hotel to do a bit of shopping before going home for the night. As she stepped out onto the sidewalk on Broadway, she noticed an older model Ford pickup rattle by and turn right on 1st Avenue North. She wouldn't have taken much notice except to check the license plate as it rounded the corner—county 7–Lake County, Kalispell, Bigfork, she observed. She had just been up there for the cherry festival in neighboring Polson. She couldn't see the driver as he disappeared east on 1st Avenue. She then walked up the street to the Hart-Albin department store.

The rattle, Landi realized, was from his loose front bumper. He hadn't noticed it out on the highway, but in town the noise reverberated, making him a bit self- conscious as he rounded the corner past the tall Northern Hotel. A block further, he passed the General Custer. In the next block he spotted a much smaller and less classy Lincoln Hotel. He found a parking place and went in to the desk. He obtained a room on the third floor in which he stayed the night. He had already had dinner at the Muzzleloader on 1st Avenue South as he came into Billings earlier.

The next morning he returned to the Muzzleloader for breakfast before heading east toward Iowa. While at breakfast he examined his map and decided that he would go south into Wyoming and stay overnight in Casper. Then he would go on to Cheyenne where he could get onto U.S. 30 which would take him into Iowa. Depending on how many miles he could make in a day, he estimated a couple more overnight stops before reaching Ft. Madison, Iowa, where he hoped to find Eleanor. *If my truck will make it,* he mused as he got on the road to continue his pilgrimage.

The trip to Casper took most of the day. At first the sky was blue and sunny, but toward late afternoon clouds had built up in the east which gave Landi a sense of foreboding. It was now late enough in the fall that snow could be expected. By morning of the next day the temperature had dropped and it was quite windy as Landi continued his journey southeast on Highway 87 toward Cheyenne. He stopped for a quick lunch in Wheatland and then headed south into more wind and black clouds. The wind began to spit snow flakes onto his windshield. He noticed that there were no oncoming vehicles on the road from the South. He wondered why, but soon found the answer. The wind and snow were increasing as he got nearer to the town of Chugwater. It was then that he saw a flashing light up ahead. He came to a Wyoming state highway patrol at the outskirts of Chugwater. The trooper signaled him to stop. He came to Landi's side window and announced. "The highway beyond Chugwater has been closed due to a severe blizzard with blowing snow reducing visibility to zero. The pavement is glare ice. A semi has jackknifed and is blocking both lanes. You can either turn around or go into Chug for the duration of the storm, and until we can clear the highway."

Landi found two or three other vehicles waiting outside Horton's Corner gas station and store. He took the opportunity to fill up on gas. A man with a slight European accent waited upon Landi. "I see you are from Montana. Where are you headed?"

"Iowa. I was planning on going down to Cheyenne for the night and then east on U.S. 30. Now I don't know what will happen. Any ideas?"

"I don't think this road will open until tomorrow sometime. But there is another option."

"What's that?"

"There's a state road–313–running east from here through Lone Tree Canyon over to Highway 85 which also goes to Cheyenne. But I would suggest you take it north to Torrington and then you can take 26 up the Platte to North Platte, Nebraska, where you can get onto 30. That way you'll be going around the storm."

"I'm game. Can you show me where I get onto 313?"

"Yeah." He thought for a moment. "But if you wait a few minutes, I'm going over there myself and you can follow me."

"That would be great."

"Good. My name's Erik Larsson. We need to hurry before any of this weather gets over that way. I will drive up 85 to my brother's house and you can follow me there before going on."

"I'm Landino Ferrini. Thanks for your help."

He paid for his gas and bought a couple of candy bars for the trip ahead. He was soon on the road following Larsson.

In a little over an hour they arrived at the home of Magnus Larsson, who invited Landi to come in. Fortunately the storm clouds remained to the south. "Mr. Ferrini, you must stay for a bit of supper before you leave for Torrington." Magnus turned out to be a most interesting host while they ate. He turned to Landi, "Your meeting my brother reminds me of how I came to America in the first place some years ago."

"How so?"

"I had been in the Swedish Navy and I was discharged in England. So I was on the docks in Liverpool, England and out of work. A bum comes up to me and says, 'Hey, Keed, do you want to go to America with me and we can ride the rods out to the West where there is a lot of work for us? So that's what I did. We took a freighter and when we got to America he showed me how to ride the rods by jumping onto a moving freight train and riding in an empty box car. We finally went legal and hired on to work on building the railroad tracks over Sherman Hill west of Cheyenne.

"Well, when I got to Cheyenne, Wyoming I jumped off and got onto a train going north—without a ticket. The conductor came along with a shot gun and made me get off. That was at Chugwater, where in those days the British-owned Swan Land and Cattle Company was headquartered. I got a job with them and finally I became manager of the Swan Land and Cattle Company! We had thousands of cattle spread all over that region of Wyoming."

"Wow! That's quite a story, sir."

"Yes it is, and all because of a chance meeting with a bum on the docks at Liverpool, England. Who knows what will happen in your life all because of meeting Erik Larsson in Chugwater, Wyoming!"

Erik chimed in, "At least he won't wind up in a snowdrift north of Cheyenne."

"That's right, and I'll always be thankful to you for that."

Erik continued, "Once you get to Torrington and you turn east on 26 you'll be going along the old Oregon Trail following the Platte River."

"Oh?"

"That's where the wagon trains came west from Missouri all the way to Oregon where the Willamette Valley promised lush farm and pasture land for the homesteaders who traveled in the covered wagons. Wagon train after wagon train during the middle of the last century. Some say as many as 400,000 farmers, ranchers, miners and others. It was a hazardous journey and some didn't make it. You can see lonely forgotten graves along the trail, even to this day."

"That was quite a pilgrimage for all those folk."

"You bet it was. 2000 miles at ten miles a day. They had to leave early in the springtime so that they could get through the trail before the snow flies, and they had the mountains to cross. A lot of the old mountain men became guides for those greenhorns."

Magnus declared, "The greatest pilgrimage in American history." He then added, "About twenty-five to thirty miles east of Torrington you'll see Chimney Rock near Scottsbluff. That was an important landmark for the immigrants. Now, if you are planning to come back this way, when you go west from Torrington about twenty miles you'll come to Ft. Laramie, which was a military fort along the trail to protect the immigrant wagon trains from hostile tribes. Another ten miles or so, you come to Guernsey where you can go out and see the ruts in the sand stone from the wagons. Also, there is a sandstone cliff along the river on which many immigrants carved their names, It's called Register Cliff. It was their first overnight stop after leaving Fort Laramie. Beyond the fort, their pilgrimage became even more arduous as they traversed the mountains and then downward to the coast."

Erik then said, "Don't let us keep you, Landi. We know you want to be on your way."

"Yes, I guess I am on my own pilgrimage. Thank you for the fine supper and that inspiring story, Mr. Larsson, and Erik for your great help to me on my way."

"I am glad I could help you on your journey . . . and, oh, by the way, do you play chess?"

"I did when I was a young fella in Italy. Why do you ask?"

"I'm always looking for somebody to play chess with. No one around here knows the game. Erik won't play me anymore. . . I beat him all the time. I wish you had time to stay for a game. But, maybe when you come back through here we could play."

"Thanks for that. . . maybe sometime, Mr. Larsson." At that Landi made his departure and got on the road to Torrington.

On the south edge of Torrington, Landi found Highway 26 and turned east to follow it through a succession of small towns. Near Bayard, Nebraska, Landi was truly inspired as he thought about the travelers on the Oregon Trail. He spotted the chimney in the distance and as he drove nearer to it and then passed it he thought about the significance of this sight for the weary pilgrims of a hundred years ago.

This triggered thoughts about his own pilgrimage. For the immigrants on the trail to Oregon, visions of their trail's ending in the verdant valleys must have kept them focused on a bright future for them and their families. *I have a vision of Ellie and I can imagine a wonderful future—if I can find her. But I have no idea where my trail will end. I hope somewhere in eastern Iowa. . . but I have no assurance.*

Landi pondered Magnus's reference to his chance meeting of an American bum on the docks in England, how it shaped the rest of his life. *And implying that my meeting Erik would be an important influence on my journey. I don't know quite how that could be?* There would come a time when Landi would hear of the blizzard of '49 in which people lost their lives stuck in their vehicles between Chugwater and Cheyenne. *That's where the Larssons made an important contribution to my pilgrimage,* he would later conclude.

Landi stepped harder on the pedal in an effort to get to Iowa as soon as possible. He made it to North Platte and then onto US#30 at mid-day. He pulled into a gas station at Kearney at nightfall. He gained permission to spend the night in his pickup on the gas station grounds. There was room in the bed of the truck to fold out his sleeping bag.

While he was preparing his bed roll, another Ford pickup drove up to one of the pumps. When the driver was having his gas filled up he stepped over to Landi "This is a 1939, isn't it?"

"Yes it is."

"Looks in pretty good condition. How's the engine?"

Landi remembered that from time to time he had worried a bit over a knock in the motor at higher speeds. "Fair. . . using some oil, though," he answered. By this time Landi wondered what the man was up to. "Why do you ask?"

"I have an auto collection which I have on display down in Minden. It just so happens that I do not have a '39 pickup. They were pre-war, and people drove them to the junk yard before they could buy anything new. . . You wouldn't want to sell it, would you?"

This took Landi by surprise. The man was older than Landi by ten years or so, dressed in bib overalls with a couple of wrapped cigars in his breast pocket. He seemed to have a very common and friendly demeanor. "I don't know. I'm from Montana and I'm going to eastern Iowa. . . I don't have any access to extra funds. . . I'd have to find something about the same price for the rest of my trip."

"Mind if I have a look?"

"Go ahead."

He walked around the vehicle slowly, looked under the hood and inside. "This really is what I've been looking for. . . I tell you what, I'll trade you straight across for my '44 over at the pump." It was Landi's turn to inspect the newer pickup. He observed that it had considerably fewer miles on it than on his. "Any engine problems?"

"No, I drive it to Omaha all the time and it is quite reliable."

Landi thought for a while. "It's a deal," and he shook hands with the man.

The two exchanged names and addresses as well as license plates and various personal items in each vehicle. It had been the custom of both men to carry their vehicle title with them when away from home and so they could complete the transfer information for filing. The man drove off in an orange 1939 model for his collection and Landi prepared for bed in his green 1944 model, which had come to him as a complete surprise, and which he hoped would serve him well on the rest of his pilgrimage.

The next morning, after a hasty breakfast at a downtown café, Landi eagerly hit the road in his "new" pickup, anxious to see what he had gotten himself into. He found himself able to travel at a slightly higher speed now, and he did not hear any knocking in the engine. *In fact she really purrs nicely. But it sure smells of cigar smoke in here. Reminds me of Big Al.*

Landi was further reminded of his Chicago days when he negotiated the heavy traffic on the streets as he drove through Omaha. Toward evening, he crossed into Iowa at Council Bluffs and went south to US 34 and on to Red Oak where he spent the night.

The next day, around noon he turned south at Ottumwa to Highway 2 and estimated that he was less than a hundred miles from his destination of Ft. Madison.

Landi arrived late in the evening and found a room in the Anthe Hotel aowntown. In the morning at a local cafe he asked for directions. "Can you tell me how I can get to 1320 Ave. I?"

The waitress gave him directions. He paid his bill and headed for Eleanor's childhood house. *Could this possibly be the end of my pilgrimage? Might Ellie be here?* he thought as he pulled up to the house. He sat for moment in his pickup uttering a silent prayer, before getting out and walking up to the porch. He rang the bell and waited nervously.

Finally the door opened part way and a woman in her sixties appeared. "Yes?"

"I'm looking for Eleanor Helm. Does she live here?"

"No. You must mean Emily. She's married to Ernest Hauser over by St. John's Church."

Landi was floored when he jumped at the conclusion that the woman had remembered the wrong name, and that it was Eleanor who was married. "I see. Can you give me their address?"

She took a pad and pencil out of her apron pocket and wrote down the address and gave it to Landi. "They both work at Schaeffer Pen and so you wont find them there until tonight."

"She sold the house to me when they married. I've enjoyed this fine old house. We go to the same church. Ernest is the organist. Has been for years. I used to know her parents, but they died some years ago."

"Well, thank you very much."

"And, oh yes. Mrs. Hauser is our Sunday School Superintendent."

"Good." *If she keeps talking I might find out about Ellie.* "By the way. are you sure you don't mean that Mrs. Hauser's name is Eleanor, and not Emily?"

"No I don't think so. . . come to think of it, there were two sisters in that family. One of them left for a while, but the other was here all along. But I don't remember which."

"Well, thanks again."

"Quite all right. I forgot to tell you that Ernest still uses my garage for working on some old cars he likes to fix up."

"O.K." Landi rushed off before she thought of something else. It would be a long day of waiting to see the Hausers after work. He waited until after the supper hour and then drove up to their door. From what he gathered from the lady in Eleanor's house, there was a degree of chance that he would find Ellie here. He met this thought with mixed emotions. To finally see her was a happy thought, but to find her married would be a huge disappointment. How would he handle that?

He rang the door bell. The man of the house answered. "Hello?"

"Hello, sir. Are you Mr. Hauser?"

"That's right."

"I'm Landino Ferrini. I am looking for Eleanor Helm."

"Oh my! Won't you come in. I'll call my wife."

"Honey, it's Landino!"

Landi could see a woman emerging from the kitchen. She looked vaguely like Ellie. *But it's been a long time.*

When she appeared, Landi was baffled. She looked like Ellie, but not quite.

"Emily, Landino, here is looking for your sister."

"Hello. Landi. Ellie used to talk about you. But she assumed you were dead, shot by the Mob up in Chicago. I can't believe it. . . .Are you really Eleanor's Landi?"

"I am. . . Hello, Emily." He reached out to shake her hand."

"Please, let's all sit down."

When they were seated, Emily asked, "How is it you are alive? I know at sounds like an impossible question."

"I escaped from the Mob before they had a chance to do me in. And I thought Ellie had been burned to death in a hotel fire in Missoula. . . but found out later that she had not been in the hotel at the time. . . and now I'm trying to find her. . . hoping she might be here."

Touched by this, Emily seemed on the edge of tears. "Oh, Landi, I'm so sorry."

"Do you know where she is?"

"Sad to say, we have lost track," Ernest answered.

"After our mother died, she left to go back to Montana." She looked downcast. "She and I hadn't gotten along. I had been resentful over her not being around to help with Mother after she became ill."

Landi added. "Ellie had been so guilt- ridden over having left the family to go to Chicago."

"Well anyway, that accounted for our losing touch again, I think."

"Do you have any idea where in Montana?"

"Only that somebody told us a few years ago something about her working in a hotel in one of the bigger cities in Montana. That's all."

"I'm sorry. That's all we can tell you," Ernest concluded.

With that, Landi, feeling quite forlorn and frustrated, said, "Well, I guess I need to return to Montana and continue my search."

Ernest looked at his wife and then suggested, "Landi, won't you stay and have supper with us before you go on you way again. Turning to Emily, "Can we fix something quick?"

"Sure we can. Make yourself at home, Landi. I'll just be a few minutes."

Over supper, Landi had a chance to hear more about Ellie's trip to Iowa and her time in the family home before their mother passed away.

Landi sensed that this conversation was a little awkward for Emily, but Ernie made up for it with his affable nature.

After supper Landi thanked his hosts and declared that he was most anxious to get back to Montana.

Returning to his pickup he thought, *Now to go back to Montana as quickly and directly as I can. My money is getting low.* He thought again of Ernest's final words about Eleanor working in a Montana hotel. *Most likely that would be a small hotel in Missoula. . .so I guess the pilgrimage goes on to Missoula again and to the Marinos.*

Peter and Luisa Marino were the only "family" Landi had, and so anticipating his return to Bigfork took on the feeling of going home again. He kept this thought as a hedge against what he thought would be a long shot to find Eleanor in Missoula. But he had to try to find her. It was all he had to go on.

CHAPTER 35

The loneliness which Eleanor had felt when she began her life in Billings had abated in recent years with the friendship which had developed between her and the Marino family–both generations--, not only in Billings but up on the Flathead as well. She had been spending her vacation weeks in a rented cabin she had found on the East Shore on Woods Bay. She had come to feel like a member of the Marino family.

She had promoted Dan Marino to assistant manager and found him to be a great help in the day-to-day operation of the hotel. But she was feeling pressure from the owners to increase her occupancy rate. The development of Interstate 90 had brought competition to the downtown hotels as motels began to appear at the 27th Street and King Avenue interchanges. The more the owners pushed her, the more Eleanor became frustrated with the market, especially during the winter months when road travel was down.

Eleanor hired an advertising agency who provided ads for print and electronic media in the area. They installed a back-lit sign to be placed in the Logan International Airport terminal building. On one of trips up to the terminal to check on the sign, she noticed a number of passenger vans, each of which carried the name of one of the motels in the area. Upon recommendation of her ad agency she purchased a limousine for transporting guests to and from Logan International.

When she reported these measures to the owners and what she could estimate the positive effect on occupancy appeared to be their response was mixed. "We applaud your new approaches to attracting guests, but your increases are not as yet adequate. We will check with you again further at the end of next month. We would like a tour of the facility before we leave, if it is convenient."

"Certainly." *it would not be convenient at any time.* She thought.

They settled for a tour the following Saturday afternoon.

Eleanor and Dan alerted her staff and everyone spent the weekend preparing for this top level tour. In the midst of the last minute sprucing the dining room staff was in a frenzy getting ready for a banquet for 250 people on Saturday evening. A sit-down, full course dinner for 250 stretched things to the limit. Adding to the stress on the staff was a Billings Fire Department inspection requested for first thing Saturday afternoon.

Eleanor was in her office during the inspection. She was waiting for the fire department report when the desk clerk bought her a letter marked "Personal.' It was from Dorothy—the first contact in years. It had been sent to the house in Iowa and then forwarded by Emily to Eleanor in Billings. Eleanor slit open the envelope and began reading about the surprise visit Landi had made to Church Hill. She was absolutely stunned. *I can't believe it. She must be mistaken. . . . Landi couldn't be alive . . . or could he be? I've got to get in touch with Dorothy as soon as possible.*

Just then one of the firemen brought in their report."Here is our report. There is a section which you should give to the engineer and another to the Housekeeping manager. Both the engineering and housekeeping departments were given lists of problems to be resolved as soon as possible. Eleanor needed to sit down with both managers as soon as possible. She phoned each and had them come up to her office. They discussed the lists of problems and arrived at a tentative plan for caring for the recommendations.

The owners were in the lobby when the fire truck pulled away, and Eleanor came out of her office, greeted them. "Welcome to the Northern, Montana's premier hotel."

"Thank you, Miss Helm. But what was the fire truck doing here?"

"Oh, they had just made their annual inspection."

"What did they find?"

"A few little things for our engineer and for the linen room manager. . . nothing major." she then let them begin their tour. She followed, ready to answer any questions they might have.

Eleanor did no better when the owners tour concluded and she was advised of some needs to be remedied in a number of the public rooms of the hotel.

As soon as the owners had departed, guests began coming in for the large banquet. Eleanor usually did not remain in the hotel for evening dinners and receptions, but for this big one she thought she ought to stay in case any emergencies arose. Earlier she had made a point of informing the owners of this large banquet, as an example of how well the catering department was doing these days.

Eleanor felt very tired as she waited for the banquet to be over. When the guest began leaving, she prepared to make her exit. Before s he could get away the chef came to her office with some complaints about the dining room staff.

"I'll look into this first thing Monday morning. I'll get back to you, Armando."

"Thank you."

One more thing to worry over.

That evening after getting home totally bushed. *Too late to call Dorothy. I'll call first thing in the morning.* Eleanor went to bed with a throbbing headache together with a vague uneasiness. Her sleep was quite fitful. Around three in the morning, she awakened short of breath and feeling quite ill and nauseated. She called 911. And quickly slipped her note from Dorothy in her pocket. When the EMTs arrived they put her on a gurney and placed her in the ambulance and took her to the Emergency Room of Deaconess Medical Center. She had thought to grab the letter she had gotten from Dorothy and she quickly stuffed it in the pocket of her robe.

At seven, Dan received a phone call while he was getting dressed. "Mr. Marino?"

"Yes."

"I'm Doreen, one of the ER nurses at Deaconess. We have Eleanor Helm here in ER. She is asking for you. Can you come immediately?"

"Yes, of course. I will be there as soon as I can."

"Thank you. I will be looking for you."

Dan finished dressing and was on his way in ten minutes, wondering worriedly what was he matter and in what condition he would find Eleanor.

He found a parking place close to the hospital emergency entrance. He rushed into the ER and was met by Doreen.

"Mr. Marino?"

"Yes."

"Come with me. Eleanor is able to visit with you briefly."

When they came into her room, Doreen announced, "Here is Mr. Marino, Eleanor." She adjusted Eleanor's pillow and got out of the way so that Dan could step up to the bedside.

"Oh, Dan. I'm so glad you could get here before they take me to surgery."

"Hello, Eleanor. What has happened?"

"It's my heart. They want me in surgery as soon as they can take me. I guess they will find out at that point whether they need to do heart surgery on me."

"I'm sorry."

"I woke up around three and felt deathly sick and so called 911. . . and here I am."

"I see. Good thing they got you here." Dan really didn't know what else to say. This was a "first" for him.

"Dan. The main reason I needed to see you is that I want you to take the letter which is in my robe pocket over there."

He saw her robe hanging in a small closet. He pulled out the letter in its envelope. He brought it over to her. "You take it. Don't read it until you are alone and I'm up in surgery. . . then I want you to be a detective and find out first if what she says in there is true, and then if it is, do what you have to find. . . ." At that point she began to weep uncontrollably. Doreen, who had been outside the entrance to the room, stepped in to help Eleanor.

The attendants from surgery came to take Eleanor to surgery. Doreen turned to Dan and said. "You'll need to leave. You can wait in the surgery waiting room upstairs. We will inform you when she will be ready to come back to a hospital room."

Dan found his way to the surgery waiting room and sat in an area without many others. A volunteer offered him a cup of coffee, which he accepted. He took the letter out of its envelope and began to read."

Dear Ellie,

It has been much too long a time since we have corresponded. We have lost track of each other. Then something happened and it became absolutely necessary to find you to tell you about it. One day not long ago I got a message from the school secretary that there was a man waiting to see me after school. When I met him he told me that he was Landino Ferrini! It was so hard for me to believe him and so I invited him to my apartment for dinner, for a chance to tell me his entire story.

He was looking for you. He had thought you had died in the Acme fire, but then later learned that quite possibly you had escaped, so he was trying to find you. The only thing I knew to tell him that I thought you might be in Iowa in your hometown.

After he left I knew I had to find you. It took me quite a while until I found through an acquaintance that you knew some folks in Bigfork by the name of Archer. So I contacted them and they told me you were in Billings at the Northern.

At this point all I know is that Landi probably went to Iowa looking for you. Sorry I can't tell you any more.

Ellie, why don't you phone me and we'll talk about this Please do that as soon as you get this.

Your old friend,
Dorothy

Dan remained in the waiting room unil he received a report from surgery that Eleanor had been transferred safely to the recovery room.

CHAPTER 36

As soon as Dan returned to his office, he had some things to do immediately. He then phoned Dorothy.

"Hello, Dorothy, is it?"

"Yes."

"My name is Dan Marino, a close friend and colleague of Eleanor Helm. First of all, you should know that Eleanor is in Deaconess Hospital here in Billings, having had open heart surgery earlier today. . ."

Dorothy cut in. "Oh, my! How is she?"

"She came through surgery and is in recovery right now. . . I was with her and waited until the doctor reported to me in the waiting room that she was doing as well as could be expected. I'll be able to see her this afternoon. . ."

"Thank you for telling me. Would you let me know after you have seen her later today?"

"Be glad to, but there is more I need to talk to you about. You wrote a letter to Eleanor which she got yesterday very soon before her heart attack. So she did not have time to even think about it much, I don't believe. Apparently, when she arrived in ER she asked a nurse to call me and have me come to see her as soon as I could. It was your letter which concerned her. She asked me to call you and see what the next steps might be to find Landi, unbelievable as it is for her that he is alive."

"I know. I can hardly believe it, and we need to do what we can to find him."

"Especially now that Eleanor is in the hospital." Dan thought further. "Do you have any idea how I might go about trying to locate Landino."

Dorothy agreed, "Yes, and the only thing I have to go on is that when Landi left my house in Amsterdam, he was headed for Iowa."

"Do you have any idea of where in Iowa?"

"To her former home in Ft. Madison. . .and I do know that Eleanor had a sister there whose name is Emily. Her married name, I think, is Hauser."

"I'll try to locate her by phone."

"Please let me know what more you find out. . . and by the way—you said your name is Marino. You wouldn't by any chance be related to the Marinos up in Bigfork?"

"They are my parents. Do you know them?"

"Not directly, but they are in the same community as the Archers."

"That's interesting. I met the Archers when I was up for the festival this past summer. . . Well, anyway, I'll get back to you about Eleanor's condition and also about my call to Emily."

Dan needed to attend to his work and also Eleanor's now that she was in the hospital. He had to put the search for Landi on the back burner for awhile. He left the hotel at five in order to check on Eleanor in the hospital. She was in her room, but still asleep. The nurse informed him that she did not think that it would be possible to visit with Eleanor until the next day. Dan got the impression that this was a bit unusual, that by this time a patient would ordinarily be awake and able to visit, at least briefly. He would try again the next day. He could not help but feel some concern for Eleanor's recovery. *On top of that I feel like I am a reluctant conduit linking Eleanor and Emily in this near impossible search for Landi.*

That evening when Dan phoned Emily he did not get any answers as to Landi's whereabouts. "When he left us, he was heading back to Montana. That's all we know."

However, his information about Eleanor's hospitalization concerned Emily greatly and she took the hospital address and said that she would be in touch with her sister as soon as she was out of the recovery room and placed in the ICU.

Eleanor remained in ICU for another week before she was transferred to a critical care room. During this time, Dan saw her when he could but found his work so pressing that he had little time for any other concerns.

The Landi search would have to be put on hold. There were no leads which he could follow. He did not hear any more from Emily. She, however, did send a bouquet of flowers to Eleanor.

Dan made calls to Emily and Dorothy to keep them up to date on Eleanor's progress.

In early November, Dan heard from his parents that they planned a Thanksgiving dinner with the Archers, and, of course hoped that he and his family could come up to the Flathead for Thanksgiving.

CHAPTER 37

Landi's pilgrimage took him to Missoula once again. He arrived in early October. Fortunately, the roads had not yet been under any snow cover. When he asked for Eleanor Helm at the Acme, he did not find any trace of her. He then drove up to Bigfork to find a room or an apartment. He needed to replenish his dwindling supply of funds and so began looking for work. His pilgrimage seemingly had come to a dead end.

After getting settled in a small apartment and having gotten the things he had stored, he turned to the question of employment. During his previous months in the Flathead region, he had used his "cleaned up" name of Harland Ferris, still wary about the Mob. He decided to use it now as he sought hauling jobs. He placed an ad in the Daily Inter Lake under the name:

FERRIS WHEELS

I'll do your hauling or deliveries no matter how small.
Courier services available.
Phone Harland Ferris in Bigfork

As a result of his ad, a local pharmacy hired him on a regular basis to deliver prescriptions to shut-ins. A small grocery began using his services in a similar way. Soon Landi was busy and earning enough to live on and to put away a little as well.

Life settled down for Landi as his new business venture began to prosper. He found a small house in Bigfork which he rented, signing a year's lease. Thoughts of his pilgrimage to find Eleanor receded into the background, surfacing only on some evenings when he was alone at home

In the middle of November Landi made a delivery to a neighbor of the Marinos, with whom he had not made contact since returning to the Flathead. When he made his delivery he stopped in at the Marinos and was heartily welcomed.

"Won't you stay for a cup of coffee so we can hear about your recent exploits?"

"Thanks, Luisa. I can stay a few minutes."

"Tell us about yourself, Harland." Peter asked.

"I made it back to Iowa and found Eleanor's sister. But she could not tell me where Eleanor had gone after she left Iowa. I don't think the two sisters get along too well and as a result her sister had no knowledge of Eleanor's whereabouts. So I came back and haven't found her yet."

"That's too bad."

"So I have settled down and opened up a delivery and courier business in Bigfork. . . and I'm doing fairly well."

"Good for you."

Luisa then asked, "We will have Thanksgiving dinner here with the Archers, and if you can we'd love to include you. . . think you can?"

"I'd love too. Better than being cooped up in my place!"

"And, if the weather cooperates, Dan and his family are coming from Billings.. . . You've met them, I think.?"

"Yes, at the cherry festival."

"One o'clock on Thanksgiving, Harland. Don't forget!"

"Don't worry. I won't. . . looking forward to it." Landi excused himself to get back to his deliveries.

The night before Thanksgiving, Dan and Barbara and Angelina arrived at Dan's parents. The next morning the Archers joined them so that Mrs. Archer could help with the meal preparation. When Paul and Beberly Archer arrived, Luisa brought out coffee and huckleberry scones. They sat around the kitchen table.

"Too bad your boss, Miss Helm couldn't come," Paul offered.

"It is too bad." Dan replied. "Unfortunately she is back in Intensive Care. I am a little worried. She should have been close to full recovery from her heart surgery by this time."

"What does the doctor say?"

"She feels that given a little more time Eleanor will be back in a regular room."

Everyone expressed their wish for Eleanor's full recovery.

The men retired to the living room while Luisa and Beverly attended to some things in the kitchen.

A few minutes before one, the doorbell rang. Peter went to the door. "Hello, Harland. Welcome. Come in."

"Thank you, Peter." he said as he entered the living room.

Peter turned to his other guests. "You remember Harland Ferris. He was here during the festival. . . and this is my son, Dan, and neighbor, Paul Archer."

They greeted each other. Harland joined the conversation in the living room after calling in his "Hello" to the wives in the kitchen.

Peter encouraged Harland to tell about *Ferris Wheels*, his new business venture.

"In October when I returned to Bigfork, I needed to find work. I had done hauling, as you know, when I was here around festival time, which isn't needed this time of the year, so I got the idea of doing small deliveries for various businesses and individuals in the area. So *Ferris Wheels—Hauling, Deliveries, and Courier Service* was born."

"And how is it panning out?" Dan asked.

"As a matter of fact, better than I thought it would. . . Once the word got around I have had calls every day since, and I'm keeping busy most days."

"Sounds great. I may have a need for your help one of these days," Paul responded enthusiastically.

Harland then gave his business card to each of the others. It was one he had printed recently with a graphic showing a Ferris wheel. As Dan took the card, he reached into his billfold for his own card and gave it to Harland. He pocketed it without looking at it, because just then Luisa announced . "Time to come to the table!"

Soon, all were gathered around the traditionally laden Thanksgiving dinner table. When all were seated, Peter spoke. "I've asked Barbara to give our Thanksgiving prayer."

Barbara prayed. "Most bounteous God, we thank Thee for all the good blessings you have bestowed upon us throughout this past year, for seed-time and harvest in abundance. We thank thee for Thy love which surrounds us and all our families. We pray for those who are ill at this time, especially for Dan's boss and for all others who must be hospitalized at this time. Now we ask Thy blessing upon this our festive meal. In Jesus name. Amen."

Peter then began passing the various dishes of food around the table, beginning with the turkey which he had carved beforehand. The festive celebration continued until the pumpkin pie and coffee completed the menu for the day.

Landi felt completely at ease during this, his first such American Thanksgiving celebration. After the meal, they retired to the living room for a continuation of the comfortably good feeling all seemed to express.

On his way home Landi felt more at home than he had since his time with Ellie before their tragic separation. Unwittingly, his decision to use the name Harland Ferris had kept him from being discovered by Dan as the "Landi" whom his boss, Eleanor, had been hoping to find. Landi went to bed that Thanksgiving night closer to the destination of his long pilgrimage than he could know. Eleanor was the only person who knew that Harland was Landi. And she was very ill in Intensive Care in Billings.

CHAPTER 38

The first thing Dan did when he returned to Billings on Friday after dropping the family off at home, was to go to Deaconess and see how Eleanor was doing. He found her in a regular room without intravenous and monitoring equipment attached. When she saw him as he entered her room, she immediately smiled, "Hello, Dan. I'm glad you've come to see me."

"You look great. I hope that is how you are."

"I am over the hump. There was one set back which put me back in ICU for a couple of days. But they have gotten my meds adjusted and I am on the mend now. . . How are you, and your sweet family?"

"Just fine. We just returned from the Flathead where we had Thanksgiving with my parents."

"How nice. . . were the roads OK?"

"Clear. Paul and Beverly Archer were there and also a local man who has a delivery business in the area."

"Who was that? I wonder?"

He began fishing in his pockets to find Harland's card. He found it and was about to show it to Eleanor when he was interrupted by a nurse who had come into the room.

"Excuse me, sir, could you go out into the hall while I tend to Miss Helm?"

"Certainly." and then turning to Eleanor, "I need to get to the hotel. I'll see you this evening. He put the card back in his pocket."

"Thank you, Dan."

He then made his way to the Northern to see how matters were there. He had left the head desk clerk, James Erickson, in charge in his place. Walking up to the desk, he was greeted.

"Mr. Marino. You're back!"

"I am. How's things here?"

"Fine. No problems. . . We had a record crowd for Thanksgiving dinner. That string ensemble was really well received. Gave a nice touch to the dining experience."

"Good."

"How's Miss Helm?"

"Quite well. I saw her in the hospital just before coming here."

"When do you suppose she will be back to work?'

"No telling how long."

With that Dan went to his office to sort through the mail which had come.

Before her visit with Dan, Eleanor had been experiencing bouts of depression, which started during her second time in ICU. Her nurse asked a social worker to visit. When Carrie Jones came in, she sat down beside Eleanor's bed. After preliminary introductions, Carrie began. "I'm Carrie, one of the social workers here. You have been having some downer feelings--have you?"

"Yes. I don't know what's the matter. They tell me my heart surgery went well."

"It's not unusual to have periods of depression following heart surgery, but perhaps you'd like to tell me what goes through your mind during those periods."

Eleanor was quiet and pensive for a while, before opening up. "I've been hurting for a long time since hearing that my fiancé had been shot. Then, later I found out that this had not happened. And so I have been trying to find him ever since . . to no avail."

"Do you have any idea what really happened to him?"

"No, that's just it. . . For the last couple of years I have gradually given up. I thought he must be dead, or else I would have heard from him. I know. . .so now when you ask why I'm down, it's like I have lost a loved one, who has died."

"Do you have a religious faith, which might be able to help you?"

"I used to. . . but I wonder sometimes if I have lost my faith."

Thinking about this for a while the social worker asked, "Would you like me to have the hospital chaplain come and visit with you?"

"Yes, I think I would."

"I'll have him come to see you."

Eleanor's doctor came in after the social worker left. "Miss Helm, you are ready to be dismissed in the morning."

"I"m glad. I'm ready to go home."

"But there are some issues I want to discuss with you first. I see from your chart that you live alone. Do you have family members nearby?"

"No. I only have a sister, and she lives in Iowa."

"I see. You will need some in-home help for a while, as well as physical therapy for recovering heart patients. That you can do here on an outpatient basis. But in-home care is another matter. If you have some friends in town who can help you at home, that will be fine. Otherwise you will need to hire some home health care for a while."

"I don't know whom I could ask."

"The social worker can help you arrange for professional home care. . . .The other issue is more far reaching. I'm afraid."

"What is that?"

"It is your position as manager of the Northern. That is a high stress job and I don't recommend it for you after the slight heart damage which your attack has brought about."

"Oh, Doctor, I don't want to let that position go. I took a long time to work my way up to General Manager. . .and the Northern is the signature hotel in Billings, if not in Montana. I started out in the hotel business a long time ago as a chambermaid in a little railroad hotel in Missoula. I can't afford not to work and I can's see myself stepping down."

"It has to be your decision. . . but another heart attack could be fatal." He got up to leave.

"Think about it, Miss Helm. I'll see you in the morning and we'll sign you out." After he left the room, Eleanor had a great deal to think about. As she wrestled with her need for in-home help and for job change, some ideas were starting to take shape. Eleanor's sleep that night was quite disturbed . In the morning, her vital signs indicated to the doctor that she needed at least another day before he would be willing to dismiss her.

The following day, the hospital chaplain came in to see Eleanor. After the preliminaries he said. "The social worker suggested that you might be feeling some depression, that might be making you question your faith."

"Yes, I used to feel confident that God was leading me, and then when my fiancé disappeared I began to doubt God's help.. . .not only that, but that God must be punishing me."

"Can you tell me more about this?"

Eleanor then shared with the chaplain her story and how she now felt that she woulld never see Landi again. She no longer felt that she deserved God's love.

In a very gentle way the chaplain helped Eleanor to gain some hope for a better outcome. he helped her to see that God wanted her to find Landi as much and more than she did. This left Eleanor with a lot to think about.

In the evening, Dan and Barbata came to visit Eleanor. This gave her an opportunity to discuss with them what her doctor had recommended. It was Barbara who offered. "Eleanor, you could stay with us until you are able to navigate on your own. I'm only working part-time and can be around the house as much as you need me. Angelina would be thrilled." She turned to Dan, "What do think? Could we do that? Don't you think that would work?"

"I think so. Unless Angelina would be too much for Eleanor."

Eleanor spoke up, "She would be fine. In fact she would boost my morale. But are you sure you both want to upset your routine and have me on your hands like that?"

"We are fine with it."

Eleanor hesitated and then declared, "I would love it. I think it would be good medicine for me. . .Now, Dan, I have another suggestion!!"

"You do?"

"I would like to suggest to the owners that you and I trade positions. My doctor feels that the stress of my job could be too much for me after the slight heart damage which I have experienced recently. I think you are ready and able to take over as General Manager, and I could very well slip into second place and let you handle the stress. . . What do you think?"

"I'm flabbergasted. . . but given the situation as you describe it, I would be willing to be considered for the position. . .if you think I can do it."

"I do, Dan, and I am glad you are willing."

CHAPTER 39

Sometime in the middle of December, Landi was looking through his wallet and came across the business card Dan Marino had given him. It included an attractive photo of the ten storied Northern Hotel and information about the hotel which he recognized from his trips through downtown Billings. When he took a closer look he read not only that Dan Marino was the assistant manager but that the general manager was Eleanor Helm. He was floored. *Unbelievable. One more day of driving and my pilgrimage will be over. After the many long days spent trying to find her. And here she is relatively close. And manager of the top hotel in Billings, if not of the state. Certainly the most imposing building as one drives through the city.*

My Eleanor: First I thought she was dead, burned to death in a fire, then when I heard she was alive, I couldn't find her. Soon I will see her again!

The next morning, Landi hurried through a few small deliveries he had scheduled. He left mid-morning for the most anticipated final trip in his long journey. Speeding along Highway U.S. 10 eastward, Landi held his foot down on the gas pedal of his Ford pickup as steadily as he dared. By four o'clock in the afternoon Landi drove onto 1st Avenue North in Billings and spotted the tall red brick Northern Hotel a few blocks ahead. He found a parking place on the street a block just west of his destination, got out of his truck and briskly walked the final leg of his pilgrimage.

Finally Landino Ferrini walked into the lobby of the Northern Hotel in Billings, Montana, stepped up to the desk and asked to see the manager.

"Who shall I say you are?"

"Harland Ferris."

The clerk picked up the house phone and said. "There is a Harland Ferris here to see you." He then directed Harland to "the second door on your right."

Harland knocked. The door opened. Dan Marino held out his hand. "Harland. So glad to see you. You must have a delivery pretty far afield."

Harland was speechless. Finally he collected himself. Disappointed that he was not finding Eleanor, he said somewhat feebly, "Hello, Dan. I was under the impression you were the assistant manager. But congratulations on your promotion."

"Thank you. What can I do for you?"

"Oh. . . I was really looking for Eleanor Helm."

"She's in the office next door. We traded positions. After her heart attack."

Taken aback, Harland asked. "Would you ring and tell her that Harland Ferris would like to see her?"

"I can do that." Dan picked up the phone and dialed her number. "There is a Harland Ferris here to see you." There was complete silence on the phone. In about a minute Dan's door burst open.

"Landi!"

"Ellie!"

The two hugged. Eleanor pulled out her ring, took it off its chain and placed it on her finger again. They were together again at their trails' end.

EPILOGUE

A few months later

A shiny new fifteen passenger van pulled up to the arrival exit at Logan International Airport on the rims above Billings. The designation on its side was NORTHERN HOTEL. Three passengers were to be picked up, a couple and a single woman. The hotel employee driving the van stepped down and walked into the terminal to the baggage claim area to look for them. He knew the single woman as well as the couple. The first one he saw was Maria.

"Buon giorno, Maria"

"Landino!" She threw her arms around him and kissed him on the cheek.

"Welcome to the U.S. I am so happy you could come for our big event. . . all the way from Naples."

Emily and Ernest came up close behind Maria.

Landi spotted them. "Mr. & Ms. Hauser! Welcome to Montana."

"Thank you. . . why so formal?"

"To give you a royal welcome to the 'ball.'" Then turning to Maria. "Maria. I want you to meet Emily and Ernest Hauser. Emily is "Eleanor's sister, and this is my cousin from Italy, Maria Rossi." Everyone shook hands and they walked closer to the baggage claim.

While waiting, Landi was surprised to see Sonny and Diana Capone pick up a suitcase and begin to walk out of the building. Landi excused himself and ran over to greet them. "Mr. Capone! What brings you to Billings?"

"What do you suppose?"

"What a pleasure to have you come!"

"One more chance to make things right! See you tomorrow," he said as he ushered his wife out the door.

That sure pulls on my heart strings. And then to think that the Archers and the Marinos drove over together yesterday just for us. Also Dorothy Visser had driven to Billings for the occasion. *I'm glad we'll have a chance to visit with all of these folks at the banquet afterwards tomorrow,* Landi thought as he returned to baggage claim and to Hausers and to Maria. *All the way from Italy–wow!*

After the baggage was retrieved, Landi led his newly arrived guests out to the waiting Northern Hotel van."Now, let's go down to the hotel where Eleanor is waiting for all of you."

The next afternoon in the sanctuary of First Congregational Church, the minister spoke to the couple, and to the gathering of family and friends as well.

Eleanor and Landino, you stand here in the presence of God and before your friends at this terminal point of a long and sometimes a frustrating pilgrimage filled with doubt and fear. Each of you has been on your own pilgrimage, as you sought each other. Now you seek God's blessing of love in the gift of marriage. You have now come to the final convergence of your two pilgrimages in this sacred moment. Each of you stands here at trail's end when you will declare your vows of marriage to each other in the presence of God and before this gathering of friends, as you vow to enter a new pilgrimage together as long as you both shall live.

Eleanor and Landi, came down the aisle joyously, and together with their friends and family made their way to the Northern.

AUTHOR'S NOTES

References to Al Capone, his origin, organization and activities are consistent with historical fact as best as I can determine. Illinois City, while fictional, is somewhat typical of mining towns in Montana toward then end of the gold mining era during the last years of the nineteenth century and at the start of the twentieth. Other towns and places in which this tale unfolds are actual. The house on Avenue I is the house in which my father grew up in Ft. Madison, Iowa. As a child I had great delight in visiting my grandparents, aunts and uncles in this grand old house.

Later in life I had the honor of visiting Magnus Larsson in his home south of Hawk Springs, Wyoming, whose story in his own words has been incorporated in the account of Landi's journey through Wyoming on his way to Iowa. Other participants in this story are products of my own imagination.

The cover photo of the Northern Hotel in Billings, Montana was taken by a long time friend, David Kimball, who also provided me with material on the Northern Hotel from the Western Heritage Center in Billings.

Once again I am indebted to Jody McDevitt and to my wife, Doris, for their expert editing assistance, to Dan and Martha Krebill for technical assistance, and to Sarah Turner of Xlibris, for her guidance in the publicaton of TRAILS' END.

OTHER NOVELS PAUL KREBILL

A Place Called Fairhavens
Harry's Legacy
Heritage Hidden
Moriah's Valley
Westbound
Return to Arrow River
Sylva
U-Turn

www.xlibris.com (tab: bookstore - search: krebill)
For book descriptions &/or purchase

Edwards Brothers Malloy
Thorofare, NJ USA
July 11, 2014